Love, Lies & Blood Ties

C.J. Laurence

Copyright © 2020 C.J. Laurence

www.cjlauthor.com

All rights reserved.

Cover Designer: LKO Designs

No part of this book may be reproduced, scanned, or distributed in any printed or electronic form without permission. Please do not participate in or encourage piracy of copyrighted materials in violation of the author's rights. Thank you for respecting the hard work of this author.

This is a work of fiction. Names, characters, places, and incidents either are the product of the author's imagination or are used fictitiously, and any resemblance to locales, events, business establishments, or actual persons—living or dead—is entirely coincidental.

LOVE, LIES & BLOOD TIES

DEDICATION

For Katie – couldn't have done this without you!

CHAPTER ONE

As Luke showered, I couldn't help but ponder over things. Last night had not ended how I expected. The fact I admitted my feelings about Marcus to myself hurt more than anything. I'd opened up the gates to hurt and emotional pain without even realising it. Now I understood why so many of my school friends spent days crying and moping around after boys.

Except Marcus had no resemblance to a boy. He owned the word man. Yet his actions, how he lied to me, they didn't reflect the actions of a man. Or did they? I guessed that would depend on an individual's perspective.

"You look deep in thought," Luke said, making me jump.

Standing at the window, gazing out over his land, caught up in nothing but my thoughts, I hadn't even heard him come down the stairs. "Yeah, away with the fairies, almost."

"Anything you want to share?"

I turned around and met his soft brown eyes, wonder flickering through them. "Nothing you'd want to hear."

He took a couple of steps towards me and then reached out, placing his hands on my upper arms. The fruity scent of oranges and pineapples circled around me making me crave something sweet to eat. His red and blue checked shirt and faded denim jeans brought images of cowboys to mind.

"Whatever you have to say I want to hear," he said.

"That is such a cheesy line," I replied, laughing.

"A line?" He frowned. "No, Cat. That's what friends do. Listen no matter what."

Friend. Right. I couldn't ignore the pang that hit my heart when he said that word. Ultimately though, he had a point. We were friends, nothing more.

"I keep thinking about last night. All these feelings I had…I just feel like such a fool. Why do men lie, Luke? Why?"

A slow smile spread over his face. "I would just like to point out here that women lie just as much as men."

I laughed. "Stop evading the question."

He shrugged his shoulders and dropped his hands from my arms. "I don't know. Personally, I can't say I've ever lied to anyone."

"Of course you haven't. Because you're so perfect."

He grinned. "I'm glad you've noticed that too."

I folded my arms over my chest and tried my hardest not to laugh. "That's not funny."

He narrowed his eyes at me and focused his attention on my mouth. "I'm sure I can see a smile trying to crack through there."

"Shut up," I said, giving him a playful shove in the chest. "You're not funny."

"Tell me that without smiling."

At that point I couldn't hold it in any longer. I burst out laughing. "Luke, stop it!"

"I'm not even sorry. At least you're laughing and not moping around anymore."

"What happened to wanting to hear whatever I had to say?"

"It still stands."

I narrowed my eyes at him.

"Well?" he said, tilting his head to one side. "I'm waiting."

I found myself laughing again for some reason. "I'm going to get changed. Then you can take me out for that breakfast you promised."

"I didn't promise anything. I just suggested it."

"Are you going to be this awkward all day?"

He pursed his lips and said, "I haven't decided yet."

Giggling to myself, I grabbed my bag of clothes and headed upstairs to change. Just as the thought of a shower crossed my mind, Luke shouted up after me, "Fresh towels in the bathroom if you want a shower."

I smiled to myself. Right now, I couldn't wish for a better friend.

***

"Oooo, are we going to see the horses before breakfast?" I asked, excitement running through my veins.

Luke flashed me a smile as he guided the truck towards the stables. "You could say."

I frowned. "Why does that sound like code for something?"

"Well the other way you could look at it would be we're taking the horses to breakfast."

"Wait, what?"

He laughed. "Two of them anyway."

I gasped. "Are we riding?"

My voice came out so shrill and squeaky, Luke visibly cringed. "Yes," he replied.

"Oh my God!" I yelled, jumping up and down in my seat. "This is like the best day ever!"

Luke chuckled and brought the truck to a stop outside the hay barn.

I looked down at my trainers and groaned. "I can't ride in trainers."

"Sure you can."

I shook my head. "Trust me, I've tried. They get jammed in the stirrups. Plus, it's a weird feeling not having my ankles supported. It makes me feel like a complete novice again, riding in jeans and trainers."

"Cat, calm down. Firstly, your feet won't get jammed in these stirrups. Secondly, you won't need your ankles supporting. Thirdly, you know you're not a novice so what does it matter?"

I had so much rushing around my brain I couldn't think of anything to say back to him. The anticipation and sheer elation of riding completely overwhelmed me. I felt like a five-year-old being told they were going to see Santa.

"Who are we riding?" I asked.

"I'm taking Silva, if he's in a good mood, and I

think I'm going to put you on Missy."

I clapped my hands together and squealed. "I'm so excited!"

Luke raised an eyebrow and said, "Really?"

I gave him a playful shove in the shoulder. "Stop it."

He grinned. "Come on, let's get the tack and head out to the horses."

"We're not bringing them to the yard?"

"No. I never do. Besides, the route we're taking, we need to ride through the field so it makes no sense to bring them up here to then ride them all the way back."

I glanced out of his window, spotting little dots on the horizon. "We're walking the tack all the way over there?"

He laughed. "Would you stop squealing if I said yes?"

I grinned. "Maybe."

"Come on," he said, hopping out of the truck. "Let's get sorted."

My phone started ringing then. I pulled it out of my pocket and threw it in the door pocket without even looking at it. Nothing would ruin my morning of riding or put a dampener on my exceptional mood. I got out of the truck and followed Luke into a huge tack room.

"Wow!" I said, gazing around at all the gleaming tack. "This is incredible."

Along the left-hand wall sat eight English saddles with eight English bridles underneath, each one had a small brass plaque above it with the horse's name on it. On the right-hand wall were eight western saddles with matching western bridles, again, all named by brass plaques. Along the back wall were eight driving harnesses, all named again.

"I don't believe in sharing tack," Luke said, grabbing Silva's western saddle. "It's a very personal thing for horses. Just because they're roughly the same build, doesn't mean the tack is interchangeable. They need to be as comfortable as possible."

"I couldn't agree more. The amount of horses I've seen with behavioural issues or physical problems because of ill fitting tack is really sad. It isn't a one size fits all thing."

"I'm glad you agree," he replied, grabbing Silva's western bridle and hanging it off the horn on the western saddle. He then took Missy's western bridle and hung that off the horn of her saddle before hitching that onto his other arm. "Ready?"

I reached for Missy's tack. "I can take that."

"I'm good, Cat. These are heavy anyway."

"I think I can manage a saddle, Luke."

He grinned. "And I think I can manage two."

I rolled my eyes at him. "Hats?"

"I don't ride with one."

"Ever?"

"When I show I wear one because I have to but otherwise, no."

I'd ridden without a hat on a couple of occasions but generally speaking, when dealing with spirited super fit warmbloods and unpredictable temperaments, I'd never liked doing so.

"I do have some," he said, nodding towards a wooden box at the back of the room. "Help yourself if it makes you feel better but trust me, there's no greater feeling of freedom than having the wind rush through your hair whilst on horseback. I wouldn't put you in any danger, you know that."

I deliberated for a moment before deciding to play it safe. Whilst Luke loaded the truck up with the tack, I rifled through the brand-new looking hats and found one that fit perfectly.

"I'd rather have it and not want it, than want it and not have it," I said, walking back to the truck.

"That's fine," he said, giving me a warm smile. "I totally understand."

Luke threw some haybales in the back of the truck. I made my way to the gate and opened it for him.

"Why, thank you," he said, as I got back in the truck after closing it behind the truck.

"No problem."

"Have you ridden western before?"

"Once," I said. "We had a lady come to the stud with a stunning Lusitano. She competed working equitation with him in western tack. Fantastically trained horse."

"Spanish horses are in a league of their own. So intelligent and majestic. But I still prefer my chunks," he said, chuckling.

"It'd be a boring world if we all liked the same thing."

"Very true."

I watched as the horses lifted their heads one by one and started walking towards the truck. As before, they all soon broke out into faster paces as they realised their hay was here.

"Am I right in thinking you're leaving the truck in the field whilst we ride?"

Luke nodded. "Yes, I do it all the time. Just makes things easier."

He brought the truck to a stop and switched it off.

"If you lift up the back seat, there's brushes under there."

I couldn't deny being impressed. He literally thought of everything. As he distributed the hay, I investigated what lay beneath the back seats. Eight clear plastic boxes, all named of course, housed the basics of a grooming kit for each horse—hoof pick, dandy brush, body brush, mane comb, metal curry comb, and a rubber curry comb.

Plucking out the two boxes for Silva and Missy, I put them in the back of the truck next to the tack. Missy and Silva stood on either side of the open back, munching on hay. I looked around to see Luke shaking out Maurice's hay bed as the others tucked into their stashes.

As he came back, I couldn't help but ask, "How did you get these two to stay here?"

A devilish grin spread over his handsome face. "If I told you that, I'd have to kill you."

I laughed. "That sounds like a secret worth dying for."

"Afraid not," he said, shaking his head. "Just my excellent animal training skills."

"So modest."

"No point in being modest about something you know you're good at."

I giggled and set about grooming Missy as she ate her hay.

We fell into a comfortable silence as we readied the horses for our ride. I couldn't help but marvel at how quiet and calm they both seemed. They munched on the hay in the back of Luke's truck, totally relaxed, eyes all but glazed over. The warmbloods I'd worked with before would stand but they were always on alert, eyes wide, ears twitching in every direction, they were always ready to go. These guys looked like a bomb could go off next to them and they'd barely bat an eyelid.

"Do you want to hear something cool?" Luke said, putting his brushes down in the back of the truck.

"Always," I replied, grinning.

He walked around the truck to Missy and touched her halfway down her side. "Her girth, from here round—" he ran his finger down and then underneath her "—is greater than the length from her shoulder to her rear quarter."

I raised an eyebrow. "No. That's not possible."

"I can get a tape measure if you like," he said, grinning.

I took a step back and looked at her. She was very short coupled, meaning her back, the area where a rider would sit, wasn't very long. As I studied what Luke claimed, I could actually see it. Her belly was so deep, I'd never seen anything like it.

"That's really cool. If she were a warmblood with this conformation, she'd be a champion jumper."

Short backed horses were a firm favourite for jumping because it meant all their power was easily held together, they had less 'body' to manoeuvre which made them great for turning on a sixpence. Back home, the stud owner, Marianne, compared them to cars. Short backed horses were like hatchbacks compared to normal horses which she viewed as saloon cars.

"You can get a mini in anywhere," she'd said, pointing at her own red classic with pride. "It's the same with short coupled horses."

I thought back to her stud and wondered what they might be doing right at this moment. A twinge of homesickness hit me like a bulldozer, the first I'd really had since I'd moved here. Then I realised it wasn't my home anymore—this was.

Luke chuckled, snapping me out of my thoughts. "You and your warmbloods."

"Hey, it's all I know."

"Well, you're about to be converted," he said, winking. "If you sort the bridles, I'll sort the saddles. They're easy—no nosebands and all that nonsense."

I smirked but didn't rise to his dig at typical English tack. I had a feeling deep down that these guys could probably be ridden in a headcollar but didn't ask in case he decided we'd do just that.

As Luke sorted Missy's saddle, I sorted Silva's bridle. I anticipated him sticking his head up in the air like a giraffe. At a towering seventeen hands, I'd have no chance of getting the bridle anywhere near him if he did that. A few of the horses at Marianne's stud did that when they were feeling awkward, or didn't want to stop eating, or just found it plain amusing.

To my surprise, Silva actually dropped his head to the point that his poll, the space between his ears, sat just above my hip level.

"Awww," I said, scratching his neck. "Such a good boy."

"Bet your Spaniards wouldn't do that," Luke called out.

I turned around and stuck my tongue out at him. "You can't compare tanks to sports cars."

He shrugged his shoulders. "Depends if you want power or speed. I prefer good old-fashioned brawn."

"I think you're just jealous you're too big to ride a proper dressage horse."

"Oh really?"

I grinned. "Yep."

"We'll see about that."

I wondered what he meant and had a horrible feeling he was somehow going to prove me wrong. I slipped Silva's bit in his mouth and settled the headband of the bridle behind his ears. It felt wrong that that was it—no nosebands or throatlatches to fuss over. The split reins were an oddity too.

"So easy and simple isn't it?" he said, the glee in his voice ever apparent.

"The real test is what control you have," I quipped back.

"Ahhh," he said, patting Missy's neck and walking over to me. "That's the key. It's not about control, it's about a partnership."

I thought on that for a moment. Marianne was an excellent horse woman, she had years and years of experience under her belt, but her number one rule was that the horse had to know you were in charge at all times. She was alpha, they were beta.

"That's…an interesting perspective."

"I'm guessing your posh stud didn't train like that?"

I shook my head. "No. It was very much treating them like children to be honest. Discipline, discipline, discipline. They step out of line and there are consequences type thing."

Luke raised an eyebrow.

"Not in a cruel abusive way," I said. "For instance we had one horse who bolted every time he was asked to canter. We had him checked out by the vet, physio, dentist, farrier, the lot. Physically, he was in top form. The first time Marianne rode him, after getting the all clear, she asked for a canter and true to form, he bolted."

Luke winced. "What did she do?"

"She let him run. She sat there as cool as a cucumber as he hurtled around the school at breakneck speed. When he started to slow down, she pushed him on. You could literally see the confusion in his eyes and that he was thinking this is weird. Every time he tried to slow up, she pushed him on again and again. When he finally stumbled from tiredness, she allowed him to stop. He never did it again."

Luke grimaced. "I see the thinking process behind it, but the main thing people forget about horses is that they're a flight animal. That means they're reactive. He behaved that way for a reason. He wasn't born thinking 'whenever someone asks for canter I'm going to bolt'. Something triggered him to behave that way. Whatever trauma caused that is still in him, it's just been forced to the back of his mind."

"Trauma? That's a strong word."

"They're sensitive, intelligent animals. They have no choice but to trust us and we ask them, continually, daily, to ignore their natural instincts. We dominate them and pressure them, make them do unnatural things. What would that do to a human, suppressing their natural tendencies and forcing ideals upon them?"

"Make them depressed or make them—" the lightbulb flicked on then "—act in certain ways."

He nodded. "Just because they're an animal, it doesn't make them any less intelligent, especially emotionally intelligent. If anything, they're more so. If a horse is acting up, look at the source, the cause, not the outcome. You don't kill a weed by chopping off the head, you have to dig out the roots."

Wow. I felt like I'd learned more about horses in

this past five minutes than the seven years I'd spent with Marianne.

"Anyway," he said. "Let's chat whilst we ride. My stomach is eating itself."

I headed back to Missy and put her bridle on, thinking over Luke's points. His ways were something I'd never come across. He considered everything from the horse's point of view whereas Marianne considered everything from the rider's point of view. I suddenly felt like my mind was going to be expanded a whole lot being around Luke.

CHAPTER TWO

After using the back of the truck as a mounting block, we were finally on our way. I could feel the muscles in my inner thighs stretching already from Missy's broad width. I knew without a doubt I would ache in the morning.

"I wasn't trying to lecture you," Luke said, as we ambled across the field.

"No, I know. You've just given me a whole other perspective to think on, it's a lot to take in."

"The way I am with horses isn't what everyone agrees with. It doesn't suit all people and I don't force it on people. What works for your stud works for them, that doesn't mean it's wrong, it just means it's different."

"I guess it depends on an individual's point of view as to whether they judge it as wrong or not."

He nodded. "Exactly."

"I'm definitely intrigued on your ideas, even after just a few minutes."

"That's good to hear."

I smiled. "Where are we going for breakfast exactly?"

"Straight down to Sneaton. There's a gorgeous little farm café there that serves the best food I've ever tasted."

"How long does it take?"

He grinned. "Depends how fast we ride."

I patted Missy's neck and giggled. "Well these guys aren't exactly built for speed."

"They can still move when they need to," he said. "Which reminds me."

I frowned. "Of what?"

"Your claim I'm jealous I can't ride a 'proper' dressage horse as you put it."

Uh-oh. I'd been hoping he'd forgotten that. I knew this would come back and bite me in the ass. "What are you going to teach me now?" I asked, smirking.

"Just remind me of the core principles of dressage."

"Ah-ha," I replied, showing him my own grin. "This I know. Dressage is a French term which means training. The idea of it is to have a calm attentive horse that is strong and supple."

"Very good. Obedience is key. Would you agree? If you're in a dressage test and have to perform a certain move at E, for example, but your horse doesn't respond until several steps later, you will be marked down, correct?"

"Yes…" I couldn't help but wonder where this was going.

"So if, for example, I asked for an instantaneous walk to canter—" right on cue, Silva sprung into a slow, collected canter "—and the horse responded immediately, I'd have good marks. Yes?"

My jaw dropped as I watched him slowly canter away from me, the motion of him and Silva making me think of a rocking horse. He turned right, cantering a slow circle around me and Missy, who hadn't even batted an eyelid.

"And if my horse extended and collected at my instruction, I'd also receive good marks?"

He pushed Silva out into a long stride, his chunky long legs swallowing the ground. After half a dozen extended paces, he collected him back into a short, choppy canter and eased him back into a trot.

"And if my horse could perform a simple leg yield—" he moved Silva sideways in front of me, his front and back legs crossing in perfect synchronisation "—or a more complicated shoulder in—" he switched sides and curved Silva's shoulders around into an impressive move "—then I'd still receive good marks despite the fact I didn't have a flashy warmblood. Is that correct?"

Trying my hardest to hide my grin, I rolled my eyes. "Alright, show off. Point made."

He laughed and slowed back to a walk, falling in at my side again. "I'm just saying, don't judge a book by its cover. Just because they were built to pull ploughs, it doesn't mean they can't do other stuff."

"Impressive," I said. "But he hardly has the same elegance and finesse as a warmblood when his hooves vibrate the floor."

"That just demands more attention," he replied, laughing. "And I actually think it's more of a show when you see a horse like this move in the same way as a fancy dressage horse."

"But he doesn't," I said, laughing. "It's like pulling up to a fancy restaurant in…in your truck instead of—"

"A Maserati?" Luke said, grinning wildly.

I scowled. "Very funny, but yes, alright. Jolene's for instance. It hardly carries the same impression when you pull up there in something like your truck as opposed to Marcus' car."

"And what's wrong with my truck?"

I giggled. "It's covered in mud, has hay bales in the back, and looks exactly what it is—a working vehicle as opposed to a…" I waved my hand around, trying to think of the best way to word it "…for special occasions vehicle."

He burst out laughing. "Ok, for one, a working man has to eat. For two, that is Marcus' every day car, not a 'special occasions vehicle'."

"Oh, stop being pedantic."

"I'm just saying. Besides, if I pulled up at Jolene's in my truck and waltzed in in my working clothes, everyone would remember me. They have nothing to remember from one more sports car to the next."

"Ahhhh, so really this is about you being an attention seeking whore."

He laughed so hard he doubled over, leaning his arms on the horn on the front of his saddle. "I can't believe you just said that."

I grinned.

"On a serious note," he said, straightening up. "There is always one thing I've wanted to do but haven't quite got around to doing it yet."

"This sounds intriguing."

He flashed me a mischievous grin, even showing off his pearly white teeth. "I've been wanting to treat myself to a nice car for a while. You know, a 'special occasions' vehicle, something to enjoy rather than being stuck with the truck."

I wondered where on earth this was going. "Right…"

"I've always wanted to walk into a really fancy car dealership, in my work clothes, in the tattiest car I can find, and then buy their most expensive car."

I burst into laughter. "That's a very strange fantasy, Luke. Most guys dream about women or winning the lottery, or maybe buying a yacht."

"I'm not most guys."

"That's very clear."

"So what do you think?" he asked.

"What tatty car are you going to drive in there with to begin with?"

"Ah," he said, holding up his index finger. "My dad left behind a little old J reg fiesta. It's an absolute rust bucket but it somehow keeps going. Actually, it runs out of MOT in a couple of months. Maybe this is my ideal opportunity to finally do it."

My jaw dropped. "You're actually serious, aren't you?"

He nodded. "Totally. Wanna come with me?"

I laughed. "Seriously?"

"Yeah, it'll be fun. I'll make sure I stink of horses, am covered in hay, and wear my paint covered rigger boots, and you can do your best chav impression."

"Chav impression? What the hell?"

"You know, slick wet hair tied back in a ponytail, big gold hoop earrings, a pink Golddigga tracksuit." His eyes lit up and widened. "Oooo, we could even borrow the twins from Joanna and make it a proper show."

I actually didn't know what to say so I just laughed. The more I thought about it, the more I laughed. What a ridiculous thing to want to do.

"What do you say?" he said, after a couple of minutes of me just laughing at him.

"I think you're crazy."

"That's not a no."

"I'll think about it. I'm not sure I wholly agree with you wanting me to be a chav. Do I really look like a chav?"

"Not right now, no, but I think you'd do a good impression."

I giggled. "What is that supposed to mean?"

"Come on," he said. "What have you got to lose?"

"Ha! My dignity."

"We won't do it locally. We'll go somewhere like Manchester or maybe a day trip down to London."

"Why not go all the way and go to Dubai?"

His eyes lit up like a thousand Christmas trees.

"That was a joke, Luke."

"But still—"

"No."

He pouted.

"I can maybe get on board with the whole chav thing, and definitely consider it if we're miles away from home, but I am not travelling to a foreign country where they imprison people for anything but breathing."

"Chicken."

I laughed. "I call it good sense."

"Shall we pick up the pace?"

I nodded.

"When you ask for canter, just kiss to her, that's the signal for western trained horses."

As Luke nudged Silva into a canter, I asked Missy too, kissing the air as Luke had said. She sprung forwards, taking a big stride, and then settled into the most comfortable canter I'd ever experienced. I felt like I was being gently swayed forwards and backwards to the point if I closed my eyes, I could have been rocked to sleep.

"Ok?" Luke asked, looking over at me.

My beaming grin gave him the answer he needed.

"Try it like a real cowgirl," he said, lifting his reins up to show he was one handed. His right-hand dangled down his leg, resting just above his knee. He looked like he should be sat in a chair, not on a horse.

I debated his suggestion for a moment before deciding to be a dare devil. I'd never ridden one handed. The most I'd ever done was release the reins with one hand for a brief moment to itch my face or something.

"There's no fancy way as such, just hold them in the palm of your hand," he said.

The split reins were easy enough. The rein on the right side of her neck passed over her withers and hung down her left shoulder and vice versa. I put the right-hand rein in my left hand and centred my left hand over her withers.

"That's it," he said, smiling. "Great job."

It felt too easy, like it should be more than that. Having my right hand spare with no job felt rather peculiar. I laid it across my stomach, but that felt odd, so I rested it on the horn, but that also felt odd.

"What am I supposed to do with this?" I said, giggling and waving my right arm around in the air.

"Just relax it down your leg, like this," he replied, looking down at himself.

I did as he said, and whilst it felt strange, after a few minutes, I began to feel at home.

"Good," he said. "You're doing great. Let's walk them now. We're nearly there."

We eased back to a walk and as I went to grab the reins with my right hand, I stopped myself. If I could ride at a canter with one hand, I could certainly do it at a walk.

"Western riding is very relaxed and calm," Luke said. "The horses are trained to do what you ask until they're told to stop. Not like English where you're constantly nagging at their sides with your legs to keep them going forwards. The self-carriage is all natural, that's why the western style has longer reins, none of this feeling their mouth garbage."

"It just feels so odd to me. I feel like a spare part, like I'm not actually riding."

"That's because you're her partner, not her boss."

I wasn't going to admit this to Luke, not yet at least, but I was actually really enjoying what he was teaching me about his way with horses. When I rode with Marianne, I always had a slight feeling of apprehension, like I was always waiting for the highly strung super fit horse to do something that I needed to react to instantly. This though, this was like going for a Sunday stroll. Technically, seeing as it was Sunday, it was.

In the distance I could see a traditional farmhouse, in better condition than Luke's I had to admit. The bricks were still a bright red, the window frames gleaming white and the ivy climbing up the walls seemed to be carefully trimmed. Next to it, a big concrete patch which a couple of tractors and a handful of Land Rovers were parked on. Then at the very edge, a small building, like a brick barn, but clearly converted judging from the windows and the white house door.

"Breakfast," Luke said, nodding towards the barn conversion.

"Isn't this someone's house?"

He nodded. "My brother's to be exact. My sister runs the café. Food to die for."

"You've got a brother and a sister?"

"Yes. Why does that sound like it surprises you?"

"I don't know. I guess I just hadn't thought about your family much. Come to think of it, I don't really know that much about you."

He grinned. "Today you learned something new. I actually have four brothers and three sisters. I'm the youngest of the lot, unfortunately."

"That's a big family. I can't imagine what that must have been like growing up."

"Have you got any brothers or sisters?"

I shook my head. "Just me. Mum always said I was enough to put her off wanting anymore."

He tipped his head back and laughed. "A little mean but I can imagine you were a handful."

"Well, thanks."

Before he could respond, a green Land Rover tearing towards us caught his attention. An old B reg, it looked surprisingly in good condition for its age making me wonder if the owner was an enthusiast. However, when he hit a bump, went airborne, and then crashed back down into a hole, still accelerating, I reconsidered my previous thoughts.

"Just ignore him," Luke said. "He's a serial

antagonist."

"Your brother?"

He nodded. "Mason. He's the first born and the eldest of all of us."

I tried doing some maths in my head but then realised I actually didn't have a clue how old Luke was. "How old is Mason exactly?"

Luke grinned. "I know what you're trying to do. A gentleman never tells his age."

I laughed. "I'm pretty sure the saying is a lady never tells her age and a gentleman should never ask."

"We live in times of equality now though," Luke replied, winking.

The ancient Land Rover hurtled straight for the middle of us, barely thirty feet away. Luke pushed Silva out to the left, creating a gap between us. Mason drove his vehicle straight in between us, no hesitation, and then came to an abrupt stop. The whole thing rocked forwards, squeaking and creaking.

"Well if it isn't my little brother," boomed a deep, husky voice. "And his bit on the side."

Being the other side of the vehicle to Luke, I couldn't see the mysterious Mason, but I certainly could hear him.

"He wishes," I shouted out.

"She's got spirit. I like her already. Hurry up, Maddy is cooking today."

"Why? Where's Marissa?"

"On a dirty weekend away."

Luke rolled his eyes. "Again?"

"Hey, you know the Freeman gene. Once we pop it, we just can't stop it."

"Mason," Luke said, his voice all but a growl. "Shut up."

Barks of laughter came from the Land Rover before he sped off, turned around, and bounced back past us.

"I see he takes care of his old vehicles," I said, trying to ignore the last comment he'd made.

"I'm so sorry," Luke said. His previous relaxed posture had disappeared. Now his shoulders were tense and squared back, a muscle in his neck twitched, and his jaw had set into a hard line. "He enjoys nothing more than embarrassing people."

"It's ok," I said. "Gives the Pringles slogan a new meaning."

He cracked a smile, but it barely reached his eyes. "There's a trough of water over there," he said, pointing at the post and rail fence separating the field from the concrete. "And some hay. Loosen her cinch and take her bridle off. They won't wander."

The faith Luke had in his horses baffled me, but I trusted his judgement. Five minutes later, the horses were munching hay and Luke guided me inside the barn converted café. It was open and airy, and the smell of bacon, eggs, and coffee filled the entire space. Around twenty tables were in here, over half of them filled already.

Luke pulled out a chair for me at a table near an open window, right opposite the counter. A single white swing door was behind it which I presumed led into the kitchen. He sat down, his back to the outside door, and handed me a laminated menu.

"My brother from another mother," Mason said, striding up to our table and slapping Luke on the back.

Being brothers, I expected Mason to have some sort of resemblance to Luke but other than the height and the dark coloured eyes, there was nothing. Mason had the body of an athlete—lithe, long legs, toned muscles, and an air of confidence that seemed to have just a bit too much exuberance about it.

"Don't call me that," Luke said, shrugging off Mason's hand.

Even his fingers were long and slender, almost like a pianists, the total opposite of Luke's shovels. Mason ran a hand through his curly grey flecked hair and laughed. "So uptight. I think someone needs a massage." He looked me square in the eyes and said, "Have you not been giving your man a massage, young lady? That's not very accommodating."

I jerked my head backwards, rather taken aback, and slightly peed off, by his direct and unwelcome approach. Before I could even think of a sarcastic response to reply with, Luke scraped his chair back and stood up.

"Shut up, Mason, before I make you."

Mason's dark eyes flashed with joy. "You'd love to, wouldn't you? Bet you'd love to get your Shrek hands around my throat and squeeze the life out of me, hey, ogre?"

Suddenly, I found myself rather grateful that I'd put my mum off wanting more kids. If this were the depths sibling relationships could go to, I definitely didn't want one.

"If you speak to her like that again, I'll bury you alive so deep not even the dogs could smell you."

"That sounds like a fun challenge actually. Shall we?"

Luke clenched his fist as his cheeks burned red. "I'm warning you."

"Oh, stop it you two," said a cheery, female voice.

I turned to the counter to see a petite brunette

coming out of the kitchen with two plates in her hands. She couldn't have been much more than five feet tall. Her sleek brown hair had been pulled back into a loose ponytail, revealing her huge Bambi like eyes glaring at her brothers.

"Hi," she said, giving me a warm smile. "I'm Maddy."

I smiled back. "Caitlyn, or Cat for short."

She nodded and then took the plates to a table behind us. Seconds later, she walked straight up to Mason and shoved him so hard in his chest, he actually stumbled back. "Leave them alone, Mason."

Mason kept his stare on Luke for several seconds before flickering his attention down to his little sister. "I've not seen him for months."

"That doesn't mean he's a new toy to play with."

"No, but she is," he said, nodding at me.

Luke lunged at his brother with such explosive ferocity, even Mason ran backwards.

"Luke!" Maddy yelled, putting her hands on his stomach in an attempt to push him back.

I scrambled up and grabbed Luke's hand. When I touched him, he looked at me instantly. "Remember what you said to me? To ignore him?"

"I won't tolerate disrespect towards you."

"They're only words, Luke."

"That's not the point."

"Hey, if he knows what buttons to press, he's going to press them. Dickheads like him get bored quickly. Don't react. He'll move on."

Mason snorted. "I'm not a dickhead, thank you."

I turned around and glared at him. "Actually, I agree. But given we're in public, I think dickhead is the politest thing I could think of."

"And given you're a lady, you should watch your tongue."

For some reason, a ball of fury erupted inside me. The blood in my veins boiled with contempt. How dare he say such a chauvinistic thing to me? Where did he think we were, in the Middle ages?

I let go of Luke and narrowed my eyes at him. "What did you just say to me?"

All of a sudden, a freezing cold gust of wind blew through the café, slamming the front door shut with a definitive bang.

The twinkle in Mason's eyes vanished. He glanced at the door.

"Cat," Luke said, putting a hand on my shoulder. "Let's just ignore him."

Luke's touch put me at ease immediately. The ire in my belly evaporated leaving me wondering what the hell had just happened. I'd never reacted like that or felt such…violent emotions. I wanted him to goad me so I could hurt him. I wanted to teach him a lesson and bring him down a peg or two.

"Mason, out," Maddy said, marching to the door and opening it. "Now."

Mason looked at Luke and shook his head. "You're crazy."

Luke turned his back on his brother and ushered me towards my chair. "Are you ok?" he asked, as he sat back down.

I nodded. To be honest, I was still a little frightened by my sudden outburst, even though it had been internal. I didn't quite know how to process it.

"I'm so sorry about him," Luke said, giving me a sympathetic smile.

"It's ok. It's not your fault."

Maddy took our orders and left us to regain some equilibrium after the unexpected confrontation. As much as I tried to engage in conversation again, I couldn't help but wonder what the hell was wrong with me.

CHAPTER THREE

Thankfully, Mason didn't return. As promised, Maddy's cooking was absolutely delicious, even better than Sophie's in my opinion but of course I'd never tell her that.

"Why did Mason call you a brother from another mother?" I asked, picking at a hash brown.

Luke pulled his lips into a thin line. "My brothers and sisters all have the same parents except for me. I'm the odd one out. Same father, different mother."

"Ah, ok." I couldn't help but feel slightly awkward. "Sorry, I didn't mean to poke at stuff."

He shook his head. "Their mum died years ago. When my father met my mother, they had no intentions of adding any more children. She already had two and my father already had seven. Still, I guess the universe felt an even ten was better than nine."

"Are they all local? Your brothers and sisters?"

He nodded. "Unfortunately."

"You don't have issues like that with all of them, surely?"

He laughed. "No, just Mason. There's always been sour grapes between us. Probably because I'm a constant reminder that his dad moved on."

"What did he expect? Your dad to be single forever?"

"Knowing Mason, most likely. He's rather unreasonable at the best of times."

"You don't say."

We both laughed and finished up our drinks. Maddy reappeared to take our empty cups and gave Luke a cheeky wink. "Seeing as you've finally brought someone to meet us, does that mean you've told her your biggest secret?"

Luke's face visibly paled. "No, Maddy, I haven't."

She put a hand over her mouth and giggled. "Oops. Did I let the cat out of the bag?"

I raised an eyebrow and smirked. "This sounds good."

"It's not a good climate to find jobs, Madeline," Luke said, frowning.

"Oh, I love it when you use my full name. Makes me feel all naughty," she said, giggling as she skipped back to the kitchen.

I grinned at Luke.

"What?"

"Come on. You've got to tell me now."

He rolled his eyes. "It's really not that good."

"I think I should be the judge of that."

Maddy returned with two side plates, two thick chunks of Victoria sponge with oozing cream and strawberry jam. "Here you go," she said, her voice all high and sweet.

"This doesn't cut it as an apology," Luke said, snatching at a plate and digging in with a fork.

Maddy grabbed a chair from the next table and sat down next to me. "Did you notice anything weird about our names?" she said, bumping my shoulder with hers and smiling at Luke.

I thought over the three names I'd heard so far—Mason, Marissa, Maddy. It took me a second or two to wonder. Not sure if I might be wrong, I hesitantly asked, "Is it they all begin with M?"

"She's a clever one, hey, Luke?" Maddy said, bouncing her leg up and down under the table.

A wide grin burst out over my face. "Am I right in guessing Luke isn't your first name?"

He narrowed his eyes at his sister. "I hate you so much right now."

"No, you don't. You love my cake too much."

Luke continued stuffing the fluffy cake into his mouth with a deep crease on his forehead.

"Luke is also short for something," she whispered to me.

"Alright," he said, putting his fork down and glaring at his sister. "Enough now. Get. Scram."

Giggling like a naughty toddler, Maddy headed back into the kitchen.

"I like her," I said, trying to control my grin.

"I don't anymore," he said, standing up. "Come on, let's go riding. I've got lots I want to show you."

"But nothing you want to tell me?"

The beginnings of a smirk tweaked at his lips. "Maybe. We'll see."

***

Luke showed me around all the farms and the land that he owned. I couldn't believe my eyes. We ambled around at a steady walk, chatting about anything and everything—except the case of his mysterious name.

He seemed in such a good mood after the confrontation with his brother that I didn't want to spoil how well things were going by potentially pushing him back into a bad mood so I left it—for the time being. I had no intentions of forgetting it, that was for sure.

My problems with Dad and Marcus seemed a whole other world away from the peaceful bubble Luke had created. Riding Missy was nothing but a pleasure and when it came to finally getting off, I really didn't want to.

"Have I converted you then?" he asked.

I debated suggesting a trade for my answer for his name but wasn't quite brave enough. "Perhaps. Maybe I need another ride or two to make up my mind."

He laughed. "I'm sure that can be arranged."

By the time we got back to his house and collapsed on the sofa, the realisation of going home hit me. Almost instantly, the relaxation and enjoyment from the day became replaced with anxiety.

"What's up?" Luke said, watching me bite my nails.

"Kinda nervous about going home. Not sure of the reaction I'm going to get."

"When are you going?"

I looked at the clock—six p.m. already. "I don't know. I don't know if it's best to leave it until tomorrow or whether to brave it tonight."

"What do you feel is right?"

"In all honesty, tomorrow. But when I think about leaving it until tomorrow all I can think about is that he'll say I should have come home tonight."

"Cat, you're overthinking again. Just go with your gut feeling. Do what's right for you. You've done what your dad needed by giving him some space for the weekend. Now this part is about what you need. He's not an unreasonable man."

I snorted. "You do remember yesterday morning, right?"

He chuckled. "Come on now, we both know there are extenuating circumstances here. You caught him by surprise with something he thought he had control of at the direst time of his life."

Tears pricked at my eyes. "Thanks for the reminder."

Moving to sit next to me, he curled an arm around my shoulders and pulled me into his side. "I didn't mean it like that. How would you feel about staying here another night and then we both head to yours in the morning? Would that make you feel better?"

A wave of relief washed through me. "You have no idea. Yes, please. Thank you."

He grinned. "How about a Chinese takeaway and some Netflix?"

I raised an eyebrow. "Are you suggesting Netflix and chill to me?"

He burst out laughing. "The fact we'll have to sit on my bed to watch it has no underlying meaning to what I'm suggesting." He cleared his throat. "How about we have a Chinese and watch some TV?"

I giggled. "Sure, sounds good to me."

Giving my shoulder a gentle squeeze first, he then let me go and walked over to the mantelpiece to grab his phone. When I told him I'd eat anything with prawns in it, I didn't expect him to order what sounded like the entire seafood range from the Chinese.

"How much food do you think I eat?" I asked when he hung up.

A sly grin spread over his face. "How much food do you think I eat?" He gestured down at himself. "It's been a while since I indulged in prawns so I thought I'd take the opportunity. Unless of course you want it all for yourself? I'm happy to order more and keep it for leftovers."

I shook my head. "I usually only have a chow mein or a rice dish and maybe some spring rolls or wontons."

"Is that all?"

I frowned. "Yeah…"

"No wonder you haven't got any meat on your bones. Good call on the wontons though."

Before I could open my mouth, he'd redialled the restaurant and ordered wontons, spring rolls, and two portions of chicken chow mein. My jaw dropped.

"What?" he asked, sliding his phone in his pocket.

"First, I dread to think how much that lot will cost. Second, how much food?"

An impish grin unfolded over his handsome face. "First, it's not up to you to worry over cost, this is my treat. Second, this is pretty much my diet. One giant order from the Chinese usually lasts me the week, sometimes more, sometimes less."

"You can't be serious?"

"Why?"

"Haven't you heard of a supermarket?"

He laughed. "Ok, let me stop you there. Men and supermarkets—bad idea. All we do is chuck stuff in the trolley that's completely irrelevant and will last about five hours max. Then we end up at the overpriced corner shop where we buy more useless crap that lasts maybe a day at the most. This way—" he pointed at his phone "—I avoid the shops and save myself a load of money at the same time. It's a win win."

I giggled. His logic had some sense but also major flaws. "Ok, what about your diet? I'm sure noodles and bean sprouts aren't supposed to be what you sustain yourself on. What about fruit and veg, leafy greens, that kind of thing?"

He pursed his lips and frowned. "Well, the chow mein has green bits in it, from spring onions I think. Oh, and the Cantonese style dishes have carrots, pineapple, and peppers in. Then there's the vegetable spring rolls. The key thing is right there in the name."

I facepalmed myself and shook my head. "Oh my word. You are unbelievable."

"Why thank you," he said, wiggling his eyebrows up and down. "And we've not even been in my bedroom yet."

"Luke!" I threw a sofa cushion at him and laughed. "Stop it."

"Somebody's blushing," he said in a mocking voice. "You look so cute."

"Cute? I'm not six." I grabbed another cushion and hurled it at him, smacking him square in the chest.

"You throw like a girl." He chuckled to himself as he picked up the cushions and placed them back on the sofa.

"I throw like a girl, because I am a girl."

He nodded. "Yes. You throw like a six-year-old girl."

"Teach me how to throw properly then," I said,

raising an eyebrow in question.

"Game on. But not with my sofa cushions. We'll save that as a project for the next time I save you from Mr Darcy, sorry, Davenport."

I rolled my eyes. "Stop it…"

He grinned. "Couldn't help it. Sorry."

"No, you're not."

"No, you're right, I'm not."

I laughed. "I can see the resemblance though. The whole sexy smouldering glances and mysterious ways about him."

Luke laughed. "I'm bowing out of this conversation before I end up with my sofa feebly thrown at me. What would you like to drink?"

"Chicken. I think my throws are good and that's why you're bowing out. Just a squash will do, thank you."

"You keep telling yourself that," he said, smirking. "Squash? Come on, Cat. You can be a bit more daring than that."

"Are you trying to get me drunk whilst locking me in your bedroom with the 'TV'?" I asked, smiling.

"Not at all. I'm merely suggesting that you relax with the aid of alcohol and should you become unstable, I will be there to help."

I burst out laughing. "What have you got?"

"You name it, I've got it."

"Strawberries, champagne, and chambord."

"Except that." He ran out of the room and returned seconds later with a punnet of fresh strawberries. "I do have these though."

"Wow, you have fruit!"

"I am partial to being a bit fruity now and again," he said, giving me a cheeky wink.

I knew this was only banter and meant in jest but at the back of my mind, I couldn't help but think how I'd feel if Marcus had this kind of a conversation with another woman. Would it bother me? I couldn't say. Although, if that woman happened to be Selina, yes, it most definitely would.

"Have you got any Malibu? Or Vodka? Or Peach Schnapps? I love that stuff!"

He disappeared again and reappeared with all three of my said drinks.

"Have you got a hidden bar or something?"

"Maybe," he said, grinning.

"Can I have Schnapps and lemonade please?"

"Coming right up."

I followed him into the kitchen, marvelling at the huge traditional farmhouse décor. Everything was wood, proper solid oak, and it harboured that delicious aged smell that historic things seem to somehow acquire. He even had an old Aga against the back wall which looked to be in pristine condition.

"You have that and you don't cook?"

"That's why I don't cook. I'm preserving it."

I laughed. "That's such a lame excuse."

"Hey, I'm a busy man. Grab and go meals are what suits my lifestyle."

"Ahhhh, poppity-ping food. You know they sell that in the supermarkets?"

He laughed. "What did you just say?"

"They sell microwave meals in the supermarkets."

"No, before that."

My cheeks flared with heat. "Poppity-ping."

"What is that?"

I giggled. "My great nan was Welsh. That's what they call microwave meals. I loved the way she used to say it when I was a kid and it's just kind of stuck."

"Poppity-ping," he said, popping the p's. "I like that better than ding-box."

"Ding-box." I laughed. "What a name."

He gestured to the microwave. "It's a box and it dings when it's done."

"At least mine is original. Yours has the logic of a six-year-old boy."

"Touché," he said, laughing.

I grinned and curtsied. "Why thank you."

"Your reward is taking the drinks upstairs."

I laughed. When he passed me a pint glass of Schnapps and lemonade, my laughter stopped. "A pint? A pint of Schnapps and lemonade? Are you trying to kill me?"

"I'm just thinking ahead. I don't want to interrupt Netfl—TV by having to come down for more drinks so I'd rather take too much than not enough."

Shaking my head, I grabbed my glass, and his pint of gin and tonic, and headed upstairs. As I wondered what his bedroom would be like, I suddenly became very aware of the fact that this would look incredibly wrong to any outsiders. Other than go to sleep at six at night, the only option for entertainment happened to be in Luke's bedroom—in the form of a TV of course. However, I couldn't help but feel guilty.

As I opened the solid wooden door, the overwhelming scent of the woods and the outdoors hit me. I could pick out fir trees for sure, and a crisp cleanliness like early morning dew. Two huge windows dominated most of the facing wall, each one open and allowing the fresh air to blow inside.

To the right, a sturdy king size oak framed bed, neatly made up with plain navy bedding. On the wall facing the bottom of the bed sat a huge TV with a soundbar on the top. I noticed the speakers hung up in each corner and looked behind me to see speakers in those corners too. Surround sound. Nice. Two small alcoves housed his clothes keeping the rest of the room free of furniture save for a large bedside cabinet on either side of the bed.

"I normally take the centre of the bed so you can take the floor," Luke said, coming into the room.

I held up his glass and grinned. "Careful or I'll drink your drink."

He'd brought two lap trays up with him with cutlery and put them down on the bed. He folded his arms across his chest and smirked. "Go on then."

I hesitated. Was he calling my bluff?

He reached out and took my drink from me. "I'll even hold your drink for you."

Narrowing my eyes at him, I took a sniff of the gin and tonic. It didn't smell that bad. I'd never tried gin, but I'd heard plenty of my friends rave about it.

"Go on then," he said. "Good stuff that is. The best. Beefeater dry gin."

Bravado took over. He thought I'd back out. Without thinking, I put the glass to my lips and took a huge mouthful, all the while staring at Luke. The amusement dancing in his eyes soon became clear as I swallowed.

A hot burning sensation, like a thousand little barbs, tore down my throat, combined with a vile aftertaste which I presumed to be the tonic. I spluttered and started coughing at which point a chuckling Luke grabbed the remainder of his drink from my hand.

"That'll put hairs on your chest," he said.

I tried to speak but I couldn't stop coughing.

"Here," he said, handing me an open bottle of water. He rested a hand on my back and gently rubbed it up and down. "That was a hefty mouthful you took. Not even I drink that much at once."

I took the water and poured it down my throat. It eased the raging fire but didn't quite get rid of the rancid taste.

"That is the devil's drink," I gasped.

He laughed. "It's a man's drink. That stuff is how you differentiate men from men."

I shook my head and took another swig of water. "No. That is how you differentiate psychos from normal people. Jeeze. That's pure torture in a bottle."

He kept chuckling to himself as he pointed at the bed. "I think after that I'll let you have the bed."

I rolled my eyes. "It's big enough for the both of us."

His jokey energy evaporated in an instant. "Cat, I really don't think that's a good idea."

"You're hardly going to be comfy sat on a wooden floor and it is your bed."

He closed his eyes and scrubbed his hands over his face. "Why do you have to make this so hard?"

"It's not the middle of the night," I said, in the sweetest voice I could muster. "It's still daylight outside."

"Cat…" His voice sounded strangled, as if his voice broke when he said my name.

My heart actually ached when he spoke. The agony in that single syllable made me want to rake my words back in. "I'm sorry. I'll shut up. What do you want to watch?"

I sat down on the bed and grabbed the TV remote

from the middle of the pillows. When I turned back around, I found Luke kneeling at the side of the bed, at my feet. Taken aback, I jumped a little, but my heart kept on jumping.

"Look," he said, taking the remote out of my hand and cradling my hands in his. "If you were mine and you were in Davenport's bedroom, cuddled up on the bed, watching TV with alcohol and a film, I'd go spare. I think I would genuinely lose my mind."

"So now you're concerned about Marcus' feelings?"

He shook his head. "No. I'm just not willing to use you as a pawn in this…" He pressed his lips together, I guessed searching for words "…thing we have between us."

"Shared abhorrence for each other," I said.

"Yeah, that."

"Whilst that's very considerate of you, what about what I want? Or what you want?"

He closed his eyes and sucked in a deep breath. "What I want doesn't even come into the equation. Of course what you want does but I still have to be mindful of boundaries."

My heart somersaulted inside my chest. A lump stuck in my throat. What he wanted? What did he want? I licked my lips and dared to ask the question. "What do you want?"

A couple of seconds ticked by. Then he opened his eyes. When I saw the longing mixed with pain swirling around in his chocolatey depths, I knew the answer right to the core of my very soul.

"Oh…" I whispered. "Luke, I…"

He squeezed my hands and whispered, "Don't."

Water glazed over my vision. I recognised the fact

I liked Luke, right on the edge of more than a friend, but I was spoken for and that was a cold harsh reality we both had to take note of.

"Can I have a hug at least?" I asked.

He smiled. "Of course."

He let go of my hands and rose up on his knees, still a head taller than me in that position. As he slid his arms around my back I sighed in contentment and closed my eyes. My head seemed to find its own way to his shoulder and I nestled against his neck, inhaling his earthy smell. I wound my arms around his middle, his width meaning my hands barely reached each other around his back.

I felt his face buried in my hair and when I heard him suck in a deep breath, I knew he was smelling it.

"I love your smell," he whispered, his lips moving against my ear. "So vibrant. It's like it's all around me, coconuts, lots and lots of coconuts."

He nuzzled into my hair further giving me goosebumps. Was I supposed to reply? Was I supposed to say something equally as sweet to him?

"I—"

"Don't," he said, his voice quiet and soft. "Just let me have this moment."

I relaxed into his warmth, enjoying the feeling of something familiar and sturdy around me. I felt safe, safer than I ever had done, and I knew the second this ended, I'd only be craving more.

In that instant, I understood why he wouldn't approach the boundaries, let alone cross them. My feelings for Marcus, although muddied by last night, were still as strong as before. It would be nothing but wrong and disgusting of me to drag Luke into the middle of this. Whatever this was with us was just something born out of insecurities and needing comfort, nothing else.

He moved a hand then and before I could even think I said, "No."

With a gentle sweeping motion, he moved his fingers up and down my back. "That's all I was going to do," he said. "I want to hug you tighter but you're so fragile."

I shook my head. "Hug me tighter. I don't care if you crack all the bones in my body." Silence fell between us. He didn't hug me tighter. "Luke, I have to say something."

He shook his head. "No, Cat. You don't. Some things are best left unsaid."

I opened my mouth to argue with him, but my moment became lost to a loud knock at the front door.

"Food's here," he said, still not moving. "This is the end of crossing boundaries, Cat. It has to be."

For some reason his words felt like an axe chopping through my heart and soul. It was as if he were breaking up with me even though there was nothing but a friendship to break. I fought back a wave of tears and nodded.

He pressed a kiss to the side of my head and then in the blink of an eye, he was up and out of the room. That was it. Moment over.

CHAPTER FOUR

I expected things to be odd after that hug but when he returned with the food, it was nothing but business as usual. We joked and laughed and shared the obscene amount of food he'd ordered as we watched The Witcher on Netflix.

"Wouldn't it be so cool to live forever?" I said, purely musing as I chomped down on some prawn toast.

"I don't think it's all it's cracked up to be," he replied, shoving an entire chicken ball in his mouth at once. "There are drawbacks."

"I don't see any."

"Imagine having to see everyone you love die, over and over again. It would be soul breaking."

"That's no different to a mortal life, Luke."

"Of course it is. It's on a grander scale to start with. The friends you'd make over the years, they all grow old, but you don't. You can never settle anywhere for more than a decade without questions being asked of why you're not aging. It's essentially the life of a nomad."

"Some people like that though. Not having a fixed place to live."

He nodded. "Sure. But it's not for everyone. There's a big difference between choosing to live like that and being forced to live like that."

"That's fair. I don't know if I could do it or not."

We fell into silence and carried on watching the episode. After I couldn't take another mouthful, I made the fatal mistake of laying on my side just as the next episode started. My eyelids instantly grew heavy and the harder I tried to fight them, the heavier they became. I decided to give in, just for a second. Or several.

The constant shrill ring of my phone roused me from my food coma. As I grunted with the effort of throwing my arm out in a lame attempt to try and grab it, I heard Luke's voice.

"What? Ok, stay there. We're on our way."

I forced my eyes open to see Luke coming towards the bed. Next thing I knew, his hands were on my body, gently shaking me awake.

"Cat, you need to wake up. Caitlyn, wake up."

I rolled over onto my back and groaned. "Tired."

"I know but we need to go. Your dad has had a fall."

That pierced right through my grogginess like a spear. I sat bolt upright, nearly colliding my forehead with Luke's. "What? Is he ok?"

"I don't know. Joanna is with him. He's alive at least."

I scrambled off the bed, almost falling over as my legs tried to coordinate themselves. I felt like a newborn foal. "Knew I should have gone home tonight."

Luke reached out and stopped me from falling over and hitting the doorframe. "Cat, now isn't the time to play the blame game."

My eyes welled up with water. "At least if I'd been at home I would have been there, maybe stopped it."

"How? You'd have most likely been in your apartment and known nothing of it."

I had no response. He was right. I glanced down at the floor as I furiously blinked away my tears. With nothing to distract my mind, I couldn't help but focus on his hands on my waist. The heat from his touch radiated through my body like a thermal wave. I found myself staring at his forearms, mesmerised by not only their thickness, but the clear definition of each muscle.

Before I knew what I was doing, I raised a hand and started moving it towards his left forearm. I wanted to touch what my eyes were so hypnotised by.

"Cat," he whispered, dropping his hands from my waist.

The spell had been broken and I suddenly woke up, wondering what the hell I'd been thinking. I stepped back and looked up at him, not sure if I should apologise or not.

"Let's go," I said.

He nodded and led the way out to his truck. Even though we'd fallen into silence, he still did his usual chivalrous routine of opening the door for me. The entire journey back to mine we said nothing. The more I thought about it, the more poignant the silence seemed to be.

As Luke pulled up around the back, I jumped out

of the truck before he'd even brought it to a stop. I ran to the back door like the devil himself was chasing me.

I burst through it and careered through the kitchen and down the hall to Dad's room. The door was open already and I could hear Joanna's soothing voice talking to him.

"Dad!" I said, running into his room.

He laid on his bed, on his back, his skin the colour of milk except for a streak of blood down the left side of his face and a painful looking bump on his temple. He turned his head to look at me just as I rocked back on my heels, shocked at how dreadful he looked.

"What are you doing here?" he said, his voice hoarse and his lips tweaking up into the beginnings of a smile.

I approached the bed and smiled at Joanna, who sat at his side holding his hand. "Thank you."

"Don't mention it," she said, standing up.

Taking her place, I took Dad's hand in mine, sucking in a breath at how cold he was to the touch. "I think we should call an ambulance," I said, pulling his duvet up over him.

"I'm hot," Dad said, making a feeble attempt to push the duvet away.

"I've already called one," Joanna said. "They should be here soon."

I nodded to her and then turned back to Dad. "Dad, you're freezing to the touch."

"I'm hot," he repeated.

I pressed the back of my hand to his forehead. Sure enough, his skin was sticky and hot to the touch. "The paramedics will be here soon."

He rolled his eyes. "Don't bother them. I'm fine."

A lump caught in my throat and I fought back

tears. I couldn't let him see how upset I was.

"I think I'll just take a little nap," he said, his eyelids fluttering closed.

"No, Dad. You need to stay awake. You've had a nasty bump to the head. What were you doing?"

He furrowed his eyebrows together. "I can't remember…"

I wrapped both of my hands around his, my instincts telling me to warm him up. Seconds later, I heard the front door open and close. Thinking it was the paramedics, I stood up to allow them access.

"Hey…"

I startled at the sound of Marcus' voice. He put his hands on my shoulders and started kneading at the tension in my muscles. I didn't have it in me to ask what the hell he was doing here. This was about Dad.

Just as I was about to sit back down, I heard Luke at the front door, welcoming the paramedics in. Marcus took my hand and pulled me away to give them all the room they needed.

A tall dark-haired man walked in, his face set into a grim look. "I'm David," he said. "And this is my colleague, Emma."

A petite blonde who couldn't have been much more than five feet tall followed him in, a smile on her face. "What's happened here?"

I looked at Joanna who then jumped into answering all their questions. From what she said, she hadn't actually seen anything, just heard a bang and found him laid in the doorway. Guilt gnawed at me something chronic. I was his daughter and yet Joanna, an employee, was the one answering all their questions. It should have been me, I should have been here. I felt nothing but dreadful. Joanna shouldn't have been put in a position like this.

I watched as Emma cleaned up the blood on Dad's face and felt around the bump whilst David asked him questions.

"I think we should take him to the hospital for observation overnight. His vitals are stable but he seems confused and disorientated," David said, glancing around the room at all of us.

I nodded.

"No," Dad said. "No hospitals."

"Dad," I said. "You're not well. It's only for the night."

"No." He said it so firmly he started coughing. "I'm not going to die in a damn hospital."

That was it for me—breaking point. I burst into tears. Marcus wrapped his arms around me and buried me into his chest. I couldn't understand how Dad could be so ok with dying. Every time he closed his eyes, he didn't know if he'd wake up again. The thought alone terrified me to my very soul. Yet, Dad seemed to not care. It seemed as easy for him as breathing.

"If he refuses to go, we can't force him," David said.

Marcus spoke, his voice vibrating through his chest. "I'll stay up and monitor him all night. If I see any decline, I'll take him to the hospital myself."

I heard the paramedics packing up their stuff and giving Marcus a rundown on what to look out for. All the time, I concentrated on the steady beat of his heart, trying to time the space in between each beat.

Turning my head, I smiled at the paramedics and thanked them for coming. As Luke showed them out, I sucked in a deep breath and freed myself from

Marcus' embrace.

"Dad…" I said, my voice shaking as I approached him.

He held a frail hand up and glared at me. "No, Caitlyn. Now is not the time."

"I was only going to say they know what they're talking about, Dad. You don't look well."

He huffed. "Well then I finally look how I've felt for months."

I bit my lip. Now was not the time to bring up yesterday morning's argument in a snide comment. "Dad—"

"Caitlyn Eloise Morgan Summers, you drop this subject right now or so help me God I will banish you from this house until I'm worm food."

My jaw dropped. Everyone froze. The silence became that profound, I swear I *heard* Joanna blink.

"I was only going to tell you I love you."

I pushed my way past a dumbstruck Joanna and a stunned Luke, running back outside and into the comfort of my apartment. I wish someone could have warned me how hard this was going to be. Watching my dad decline on a daily basis had become the equivalent of my own cancer, eating away at my soul. My heart physically ached every day, a heavy dread sat in the middle of my chest, having pieces shredded off of it on an hourly basis.

Right now, I had no idea how the hell I was going to get through this.

CHAPTER FIVE

When a soft knock sounded at my door, I expected it to be Marcus. However, when I saw Luke's grimace staring back at me, I couldn't ignore the relief I felt.

"Marcus is talking to your dad, trying to calm him down I think," he said, closing the door behind him.

I walked back to my bed and threw myself on it, staring up at the ceiling. "Why is life such a bitch?"

He gave a light chuckle. "Sometimes she's good, sometimes she's bad."

"I obviously did something really wrong in a previous life. No one deserves to go through this, Luke. I never thought emotional pain could physically hurt but it does, it really does."

He sat on the bed next to me, making the wooden frame creak under his weight. He grabbed my hand and sighed. "It'll get better, Cat, I promise. Time heals all wounds."

I shook my head. "No, it doesn't. Time just makes it easier to live with."

"When did you become so philosophical?"

I couldn't help but grin. I turned my head and looked at him. "We had to have my childhood dog put down when I was twelve. I literally felt like I'd lost a limb. I cried for weeks. He was my best friend."

Luke's lips twitched. "You're comparing the loss of your father to the loss of a dog?"

"That was really traumatic for me and I still miss him now. What the hell do you think losing my dad is going to do to me?"

He squeezed my hand. "Don't dwell on it. You're souring the time you do have left with him by thinking about when he won't be here." He cleared his throat. "Do you want something to make you smile?"

"If this is another corny joke, it's really not going to work."

"Meredith."

I frowned. What did he mean? Then the penny dropped. I sat bolt upright and covered my mouth with my hands. "No…"

He lifted an eyebrow and nodded.

I burst out laughing. I laughed so hard I actually snorted. By the time I regained any sort of composure, I had stitch in both my sides and my jaw ached. "But…" I laughed again "…it's a girl's name."

"Nowadays, yes, it is. Traditionally speaking, it's actually a unisex name and back in the day was given more to boys than girls."

I giggled. "That justifies nothing."

"I'm so glad I shared this secret of mine with you."

"You wanted to make me smile."

He grinned. "Well, that definitely worked."

"So where did Luke come from?"

He pulled his lips into a thin line. "My middle name."

I raised an eyebrow. "Which is?"

"Hey, I gave you Meredith. That's enough for today."

I poked him in his side, just under his ribs. I expected the normal reflex of most people, bending away and complaining how it hurt. Instead, I found my fingertip nearly bending back on itself. How could he be so solid?

"Lucius," he said.

I sat up, trying to hide the fact I was nursing my bent finger. "That's not that bad."

"Meredith Lucius?" he said, snorting. "Come on."

I pressed my lips together, hiding a grin. "Kinda sounds like Meredith Lucious."

He stared at me with a blank face. "Thanks, Cat."

"At least," I giggled. I couldn't say what I wanted to say without laughing. I sucked in a deep breath and started again. "At least if you wanted to do drag you've already got the name."

"Good night, Cat," he said, standing up.

I burst out laughing. "Oh, come on. If this was the other way around you'd be doubled over with laughter."

"You mean if your name was Meredith?"

"Very funny, you know what I mean." I gasped. "Oh my word. You know that thing you've always wanted to do, driving in some posh garage in a rotten old car? You've got to give them your real name. It would make it sooooo much funnier."

He folded his arms over his chest and cocked his

head to one side. "I'm sorry, you actually think I'm going to willingly tell someone my real name?"

"You just did."

He rolled his eyes. "You're different."

"Tell them you'll give them X amount as a tip if they don't laugh at your name."

Mischief twinkled in his eyes. "That's not a bad idea…I like that…"

"Glad to be of service," I said, grinning.

"Only if you come with me though."

I groaned. "I'll think about it." I patted the bed and looked up at him. "Sit, please."

His lips twitched at the hint of a smile. "Only if you promise to quit mentioning my name."

"Well, that's a big ask…"

He narrowed his eyes at me, smiled, and sat down. "What's up?"

"Why…" I sucked in a deep breath "Why did you ring Marcus?"

He looked away and sighed. "Because I knew you'd need some comfort."

"And I couldn't have gotten that from you?"

"Cat," he whispered, closing his eyes. "That wouldn't have been right, and you know it."

I pulled my lips into a thin line. Deep down I knew he was right. I'm not sure what irritated me more—the fact I couldn't hug Luke or the fact he'd correctly taken the high road.

"You could have at least warned me," I said in a feeble attempt to claim some standing.

"I didn't call him until we got here. By that point you were with your dad."

I frowned. "Ok, fine, you win. I'm not going to forgive you for this just yet though," I said, smirking.

"And why would that be?" he asked, quirking an eyebrow up.

"Because I've now got to have an awkward conversation."

"Ah. You mean fix the lovers tiff you had last night?"

When he said 'lovers' my stomach jumped and my heart fluttered. Of course, nothing like that had happened yet but the implication of it made me feel all sorts of odd things.

"We're not technically lovers you know," I said, my voice quiet. I could feel my cheeks burning with embarrassment.

"I know. I just wanted to poke fun," he replied, grinning.

"Alright, *Meredith*, be careful."

"I can't believe you just said that."

"Well believe it 'coz it just happened."

All of a sudden he lunged at me, a mischievous grin on his face, and outstretched arms. When he started tickling my sides, I screamed and burst into laughter.

"Luke, no!" I yelled, wriggling off the bed to escape him.

I ran across the room, somewhat debilitated by my laughter, and soon found myself doubled over, resisting the urge to pee, as Luke mercilessly tickled my sides.

"What the hell is going on?"

We both instantly stopped, all joy evaporated as the frivolous activities ceased. Luke backed away from me allowing me to stand up straight. The aching grin on my face turned into pressed lips and a disgraced look. I felt like a naughty schoolkid who'd been caught messing around in class.

"I'm going to leave you two to it," Luke said, holding his hands up. "If you need anything, Cat, just ring me."

I nodded. "Thank—"

"She has me for that," Marcus said, glaring at Luke.

Luke flickered his eyes over to me for a brief second. He tweaked his lips into the barest of smiles and then left.

I folded my arms over my chest and stared at Marcus. "Well that was rude."

He narrowed his eyes at me, their sapphire depths glistening with anger. "Ruder than walking in on another man touching my woman?"

My jaw dropped. "First of all, don't try and make it sound like something it wasn't. He was tickling me, Marcus, you know, that fun thing that people do. Secondly, don't talk about me like I'm some kind of possession. I'm a person, not a thing."

His eyes softened and he seemed to deflate ten inches. "I'm sorry. I just…you know how I feel about him."

"That's your issue, not mine. Don't project your problems onto me and expect me to carry them too."

"Ok, I apologise." His lips curved up into a wicked grin. "But can I say I told you so when he proves me right?"

I gave a half-hearted giggle. "He won't."

"We'll see."

"Marcus…"

"I'm sorry," he said, holding his arms out. "I'm just glad you're talking to me, even if you are mad at me."

I softened slightly. "Well, I guess nearly a day is long enough. Unless you disagree?"

"Me disagree with you?" He walked towards me and settled his hands on my hips. "I wouldn't dare."

"Well that's a good thing," I said. "At least you know your boundaries."

He grinned. "I've missed you."

"That's cheesy. It's been like twenty-four hours."

"It's felt like an eternity."

I rolled my eyes. "Come on, quit the corny lines."

"Ok, you got me." He slid his hands from my hips and took both of my hands in his. A serious shadow overtook his face. "I really am so sorry, Caitlyn, I've no idea what possessed me to even let you wear that dress."

I pursed my lips and looked up at him from beneath my lashes. "Why didn't you just tell me?" I whispered, tears beginning to form in my eyes.

"You looked…there were no words to describe you, Caitlyn, amazing, incredible, so beautiful. I felt so lucky that a woman who could look like that was on my arm. It wasn't about me trying to turn you into *her*. I would never do that. You are your own person. Out of all the dresses in my sister's wardrobe, I didn't expect you to pick that one."

His eyes were so imploring, so full of honesty and care, my defences were rapidly breaking down.

I squeezed my eyes shut for a brief moment. "I just wish you'd told me, Marcus. What must your family have thought?"

He looked away and licked his lips. "My father scolded me as if I were a naughty three-year-old. He was horrified. Several of my aunts and uncles had similar opinions. They put me in my place but by that time you'd already gone." He looked back at me. "It was a stupid mistake and I swear to you I will never hold anything back again. I promise."

He lifted my hand to his mouth and brushed a delicate kiss across the back of it, giving me goosebumps. I shivered and relished the feel of his skin on mine once more. I couldn't explain it, he was like a drug to me, something I couldn't stop from wanting once he was in front of me.

"I'm sorry I involved Luke. I just…I needed to get out of there."

He instantly tensed. A muscle in his neck twitched. "I'm going to ask you one question and I would appreciate your complete honesty. Regardless of whether I will like the answer or not."

I knew what was coming but I played along anyway. "Ok."

"Did anything…has anything ever happened between you and him?"

"No…" I pulled my lips into a thin line. "We are just friends. He's very respectful of our relationship."

Marcus snorted. "Sure."

"He is." I decided to go full blown honest with him. "I fell asleep on his sofa and had a bad dream. I woke up screaming, covered in sweat. To cut a long story short, the sofa was a sofa bed and when he made it for me, I asked him to stay with me in the bed, in case I had another nightmare. I wanted comfort and reassurance, nothing else." His grip on my hand tightened. "But Luke said no. He felt that was crossing boundaries, so he slept on the other sofa instead."

"I almost want to say that's admirable of him," he said, through gritted teeth. "Why turn to him of all people?"

"My nightmares have been getting worse and whenever I wake up, I'm alone. I just…for once wanted something familiar and soothing to wake up to instead of a dark room and the sound of my own screams."

He clasped his other hand over mine, completely encasing it. "I'm sorry. I didn't realise they'd gotten that bad. Why didn't you just ask me to stay with you? You know I would have done."

"I shouldn't have to ask. It should be an obvious thing. You know I have nightmares."

"I never realised they bothered you that much. You don't really talk about them so I thought they were inconsequential."

"Well they do bother me, a lot. Some nights I wake up crying, others screaming. It would just be nice to have a hug. That's all I wanted when I asked Luke."

"My beautiful Caitlyn," he breathed, moving his hands to cup my face. "I'm so sorry. I never meant to be such a…let down. All you need to do is tell me what you want from me and I'll do it, no questions asked."

I nodded.

"Can I kiss you now?"

I grinned. "I suppose."

He leaned down and pressed his lips to mine, firm yet tender. I sighed contentedly and reached for him, curling my hands around his neck. He deepened the kiss, making me putty in his hands in an instant. Guilt riddled me as I wished we'd done this last night. Damn my mother and her stubborn genes.

I broke the kiss after a minute or so and said, "I hate to kill the passion and all that, but I think you need to finish telling me about Tatiana."

He grinned at me. "Really?"

"I need to know about my competition."

He laughed. "There is no competition."

"Oh come on. It's standard. Exes are always a threat."

"Then we need to have a conversation about yours, hmmm?" He raised an eyebrow.

"Don't spin this around on me."

"Ok, we'll leave it for now, but I haven't forgotten." He tapped the side of his head and grinned. "What do you want to know about Tatiana?"

"You said she was human."

He nodded. "Yes, she was and I liked it like that. I wanted things to stay that way but she…she had other ideas."

"She wanted you to turn her?"

"Yes. She tried every trick in the book to get me to do it, including slitting her own throat." He visibly winced. "She ran a blade across her throat right in front of me as we sat down to eat one night. She knew I'd have no choice but to give her my blood to heal her wound but the rate at which she was losing blood meant she would die." A small smile crossed his lips. "She was wily, always intent on getting her own way. She'd planned it so carefully, almost to mathematical precision. Except what she didn't expect was my reaction."

I frowned, adrenaline pulsing through me at hearing his sad story. "What did you…do?"

He hung his head, as if ashamed by his previous behaviour. "I held her in my arms as she died."

I almost choked on my sharp intake of breath. "You…you didn't give her your blood to save her?"

"I couldn't," he cried. "I wouldn't wish this life on my worst enemy. You humans, you think it's all so easy to live forever, to be invincible, but with all the pros come as many cons. I was not going to subject the love of my life to what I considered to be a curse."

"Wow," I said, surprised to find a film of tears covering my eyes. "That's intense."

"That's not the end."

I hesitated. What? "It's not?"

He shook his head. "She'd taken steps beforehand. See, she'd met my cousin, Gordon, earlier that day and he'd convinced her that I didn't love her. Combined with what she wanted and what I refused to give her she was inclined to believe him. He set the whole thing up, put the plan inside her head…but not before he gave her a good dose of his own blood."

My hand flew to my mouth. "So she…turned?"

"Three days later, after I thought I'd laid her to rest in the chapel, she stormed back through my door. She threw her ring back in my face and made a promise right there and then that if I ever fell in love again, she would turn them right in front of me."

I was speechless. I didn't know what to say. What a story.

"Gordon will go back to her and tell her about you. She's incredibly vindictive and knows how to hold a grudge. If she thinks I'm even remotely interested in a woman, she will come for them. She's been waiting for this for three hundred years."

My jaw dropped. A nervous energy overtook my body and I started trembling. "She's…she's still alive?"

"Very much so. I don't know what contact she has with Gordon. I suspected they were an item for a while after it all happened, but I can't be certain. Obviously my relationship with Gordon is pretty much non-existent."

"Where…where is she?"

"Last I heard, she took off to Romania."

Panic gripped me harder by the second. "When did you hear that?"

"A few weeks after it happened. I've done a good job of blocking her from my memories since then."

Icy spikes of fear lodged in my chest. Was this it? Was this going to be my grisly end? "In other words, you haven't got a clue where she is?"

He grimaced and shook his head. "As much as I want to keep you away from me, I'm also the only person who can protect you from her. I don't…" he scrubbed his hands over his face "…I don't know what to do for the best."

I shrugged my shoulders and tried to look on the bright side, to be optimistic, like Dad. "Maybe you're just being over cautious. Maybe she won't bother after all this time."

He raised an eyebrow. "You don't know her like I do. She won't let this go for as long as she lives."

"So what are you saying?"

He held his arms wide open, inviting me in for a hug. "I'm saying that for now, you're not leaving my side, ok? Until I figure out the next best move in this game I'm now playing, you're with me, twenty-four-seven."

My heart wanted to swell at his protective words, my soul wanted to feel warm and safe, but instead I felt nothing but ice-cold fear, sheer terror at the unknown and what may be my untimely, grisly demise.

I dared to let myself wonder if his actions meant that he cared for me deeper than what he would admit. Did he love me? Was this the reason why he hadn't said the words I knew he wanted to say? I could see it in his eyes whenever he looked at me, yet he always held back, never declared the new boundaries of our relationship.

Or was I just a desperate human, a pathetic young girl hooked up on some older guy, making mountains out of molehills, throwing everything out of perspective?

CHAPTER SIX

Marcus stuck to his word. He didn't leave my side. Even when I said I wanted a hot bubble bath, he ran the bath for me, somehow made the bubbles a foot high, then asked if he could sit in the bathroom with me.

"I…well, we've kind of not even seen each other naked yet," I said, my cheeks burning with awkwardness.

"If you're uncomfortable with it, that's fine. I just thought we could chat that's all, instead of being in separate rooms."

I pressed my lips together and looked at the mountain of bubbles. "Ok. Let me get in the bath first, then you can come in." A wicked thought crossed my mind. "On one condition."

He raised an eyebrow as he tweaked his lips into a smirk. "This sounds ominous."

"All I'm thinking is that if I'm going to be in there naked," I said, pointing at the bathtub. "Then it seems only fair that I get to look at something too."

His smirk changed into a grin. "You want me to sit in here naked with you?"

My entire body flushed with heat just at the thought, but I shook my head. "You've seen me in my underwear," I said, my temperature rising by ten degrees as I thought about that night in his bed. "But I haven't even seen you with your shirt off. It seems only fair that I get to ogle like you did."

A gentle laugh sounded from him, filling the room with happiness. "I must warn you first though."

I frowned. "Of what? Do you sparkle or something?"

"No," he said, chuckling. "If you faint at the sight of my godly body, it's at your own risk."

I burst out laughing. "Ok, Ryan. I'll bear that in mind."

"Ryan?"

"Ryan Gosling."

"He's blonde, Caitlyn."

"Have you seen Crazy, Stupid, Love?"

He shook his head.

I whipped my phone out of my pocket and brought up YouTube. I searched for the one scene that had literally made me gasp and say 'oh my god' out loud the first time I saw it.

"Watch this," I said, holding my phone out to Marcus.

I studied him as he watched it. His eyes twinkled with life, a soft edge lining the corners of them. His pink lips were slightly parted and I found myself craving to kiss them. He looked peaceful, serene, and I wondered if I would ever get to watch him sleep.

"I agree," he said, handing my phone back to me. "He's photoshopped."

I laughed. "He so isn't. Anyway, my point is, I didn't faint at that so I think I can handle seeing you."

He pulled me into him and tilted my chin up. "My dear Caitlyn. Seeing something on a screen is entirely different to seeing it in real life. But I take your point. Just bear in mind you have been warned."

I grinned. "Thank you for the concern for my health again but I'll be fine."

He pecked my lips and then said, "Let me know when you're ready."

I smirked and shooed him out of the door. As I undressed, I couldn't help but wonder what he would look like. Would he be a Ryan Gosling or something better? Was it even possible for vampires to have a stunning physique? It's not like they could benefit from protein shakes or red meat.

Slipping under the bubbles, my mind played with the idea of placing the bubbles strategically to tease him. Just a glimpse of flesh here and there. I loved the way he looked at me that night at his. I'd never had anyone look at me like that.

"I'm ready," I said, chickening out of the peep show idea. I covered myself up to my neck with thick layers of bubbles.

As I laid my head back against the rolled edge of the bathtub, I turned my head to the left to watch the door open and waited for his grand entrance. Fizzy tingles shot all the way around me as the anticipation rose to the point I almost laughed with nervousness.

When the brass door handle finally moved, I held my breath. When the door opened, I bit my lip.

However, when I saw Marcus, I couldn't help but say, "Wow."

My entire body turned to jelly which meant that my legs gave way and I slipped beneath the water. I came up seconds later, spluttering for air and coughing, furiously wiping water out of my eyes just so I could see him again.

"Are you ok?" he said, coming to the tub, chuckling.

I nodded. "Yes. Stand back over there," I said, pointing to the doorway. "I'm not finished ogling."

He obliged, a beaming grin on his handsome face.

This incredible man before me made Ryan Gosling look like an every day average bloke. Every millimetre of him was so defined I'd never seen anything like it. Not even on a poster or in a film.

"Are you wearing make up?" I asked, squinting my eyes at his body.

His skin looked as soft as snow, it almost seemed to glisten under the lights and the way it moved with each steady breath he took made me think of ice cream for some reason. He didn't have a six pack, he had an eight pack, and every single inch looked like it had been stuck on him. I could see every muscle, taut and defined, beneath his smooth skin. Even his shoulders and arms, every sinew was visible.

"What do you mean am I wearing make up?"

"That...you're...so defined. You must be wearing make up to create shadows or something."

He laughed. "I'm afraid not. This is *au natural*."

"I've never seen anything like..." I waved my hand in his general direction "...well, you, that."

My eyes kept lingering on the V that pointed down and disappeared beneath his jeans. He must have caught that because he decided to pop the button open with a wicked grin.

"Did you seriously just do that?" I asked.

"I think I seriously just did," he replied, smirking.

I scowled and turned my attention to the ceiling. "That's it. No more attention for you."

"May I take a seat now then if you're done ogling?"

"Sure, whatever," I said, waving my hand dismissively and trying to sound nonchalant.

He chuckled and sat down on the floor, leaning his head back against the wall. I couldn't help but give in and look at him. Thankfully, he started a conversation about the rest of the evening at the ball which relaxed me somewhat, especially when he detailed all the things his family said to him. After that mild entertainment, I started quizzing him some more on vampire things.

"What cool things can you do other than run fast and compel people?"

"You missed the strength," he said, flashing me a cheesy grin.

I rolled my eyes. "Other than the normal, is there anything else you can do?"

"If I tell you this, I'll have to kill you."

I grinned. "That sounds intriguing."

He laughed. "I guess I can spare you on this occasion. This only applies to born vampires. Made vampires are nothing but what TV and film depict. All born vampires have the ability to absorb and reuse magic."

"What do you mean?"

"Providing it isn't water based, of course. Say for instance I had a fight with a witch—"

"Witches are real?"

He chuckled. "Yes, Caitlyn. They are very real. Isis was a powerful witch, remember?"

"You said Goddess."

"And what powers do they possess?"

The lightbulb flicked on. "That hadn't even dawned on me."

"There are a lot of them. They're not as rare as you might think."

"Do you know any? Do I know any?"

"I do, yes. I'm not at liberty to answer if you do I'm afraid."

"Why?"

"Because if they wanted you to know their secret then they would tell you themselves. The first rule of our world is that no one outs anyone to the outside world."

I hadn't really thought of Marcus' world being any bigger than a handful of vampires. Now witches were involved too, it suddenly seemed like this was literally an entire society that lived among humans, silently.

"Ok, that's fair. I understand. So how big exactly is this world you live in?"

"Huge. It runs right alongside humans."

"Wow. Is it just vampires and witches?"

He grimaced.

"Right. Not at liberty to say?"

He nodded. "I'm sorry, Caitlyn, but the world we live in has only survived because of its secrecy. Our Elders are very strict about this."

"Elders?"

"They are the ones in charge. Similar to humans and presidents and kings, etcetera. We have our own laws to abide by as well as human ones."

"That sounds really dull and boring. Where's the freedom? Why don't you want humans knowing about you?"

"Because all they'd do is freak out there are more powerful beings than them and kill us."

"But you have all the power. You could wipe out the whole of humanity in a matter of days."

He nodded. "Yes, of course we could. But then where's the food source? Or sacrifices for the witches?"

I jerked my head back. "Sacrifices?"

"Unfortunately, it's a real thing."

"Wow. I feel like my head is going to explode."

He chuckled. "It's a lot to take in."

"What were you saying before, about vampires reusing magic or something?"

"Right, yes. Obviously the only people who can create and use magic are witches. There are frictions between the species, as you'd expect, and there are a high number of occasions where they use their magic against us. However, there's a catch."

"I like the sound of this," I said, grinning.

"A witch can bring a made vampire to his knees within seconds, much like on fictional shows. However, born vampires are a different breed. We already have magic in our blood so they can't wield their power over us so simply, much to their disgust."

"But they can do something?"

"Every witch has a basic element they can control. The majority of them are single elementals. Only a handful of bloodlines have the ability to control two or more. Water isn't a common one, unfortunately for them. The most popular are fire and air. Earth is about as rare as water. If they use their elemental abilities to attack a born vampire, all they do is give us more power. It's like getting a power boost."

Instantly, the dream I had at Marcus' house sprung to mind. Before I could stop myself, the question slipped out. "Who's Katherine?"

He frowned, a deep crease settling in his perfect skin. "Katherine?"

"The night you took me to Jolene's, when I slept at yours, what made me wake up at silly o clock was a dream I'd had. It was you chasing me, except I wasn't me. She, I, whoever, had blonde hair and she threw a fireball at you. Then she fell off a cliff."

His entire face changed. He jumped to his feet and rushed to my side quicker than I could blink. "Are you telling me the truth?"

I nodded. "Yes." I then proceeded to tell him every detail I remembered about the dream. "When I fell back off the cliff, the fall is what woke me up. I was so freaked out and you'd gone. That's why I called Luke. I just needed someone around me. That and I thought you'd dumped me."

"Caitlyn, that wasn't a dream." He leant into the bubbles and picked my hand up. "That actually happened. Word for word exactly as you described it."

I didn't know what to say. I didn't even know how to process the possible meaning of it.

"That happened a very long time ago," he said. "Sixteen-forty-eight to be exact."

"But that wasn't your mum?"

He shook his head.

"So who else am I connected to then? Is this doppelganger thing more than what you said?"

"I don't know. I need to find answers—for you and me."

I pressed my lips together for a moment and then asked the inevitable question. "Who was she?"

"Forgive me, for what I'm about to say. You must understand I haven't always been as you know me."

I nodded.

"She was just another meal. Unfortunately, I was a little off my game and she got away from me."

"Did she die?"

He smirked and pressed a gentle kiss to the back of my hand. "Oh no. She survived. In fact, you've met her."

I frowned. "When? Who?"

"Selina."

CHAPTER SEVEN

I gasped. "Wait, what? Selina was, is, Katherine?"

He nodded.

"She's a witch?"

He pulled his lips into a thin line. "Was."

"I remember you saying now that she's not human. What is she?"

He closed his eyes and sighed. "That was a slip of the tongue I shouldn't have let happen. I was hoping you'd forgotten about that."

I grinned. "Sorry to disappoint."

He opened his eyes, his sapphire blue depths alive with tenderness. "My sweet Caitlyn, you never disappoint."

My heart skipped a beat. "So what is she?"

"If I tell you this, you must not, under any circumstances, reveal to anyone that you know. I am merely telling you so you can put closure to your dream. Do you understand?"

I motioned a zip being pulled close across my lips.

"Selina is a siren."

"No! Really?"

He nodded. "The bottle of wine that she sent to me that night at Jolene's wasn't one she took from me."

"Ok…"

"After she fell into the sea, I thought nothing more of her. As far as I was concerned, she was just another witch who had plummeted to her death. It was when I was at that vineyard that I discovered Katherine had in fact survived and become something else. She renamed herself because she considers this life a rebirth."

"Are there a lot of them—sirens?"

"Depends what you consider a lot. There's at least one that permanently resides in every coastal town or city across the globe."

I couldn't quite process this, it seemed so surreal. "That's…wow. But how come she can walk on land? Sirens live in the sea."

"Sirens can't lure sailors to their deaths like the old days. Modern ships and fisherman's tales have ruined that somewhat for them. Instead they come on land, seduce their prey, and entice them into the sea."

"That is so cool."

Marcus raised an eyebrow. "Tempting someone to their death is cool? Should I be worried about you?"

I giggled. "Just the way it works is fascinating. I have to ask though, what do sirens, you know, eat? Or do they drink the blood?"

He cleared his throat. "They don't drink blood, no. They eat the heart and the liver and discard the rest."

A violent shiver ran down my spine. Something about the way he said 'discard' really bothered me. It was almost as if he were talking about a dead animal.

I gasped.

"Are you ok?" he asked, rubbing his thumb across the back of my hand.

"I…you basically treat humans like we treat animals for slaughter…" I shivered again "…it's rather chilling."

"Unfortunately, yes. But just like with animals, nothing gets wasted."

"That doesn't make it better, Marcus," I said, shaking my head. I frowned. "What do you mean nothing gets wasted?"

"Well there are fish in the sea, Caitlyn. Fish aren't too fussy about what goes in their mouths you know. If it fits, it goes in."

Something didn't quite sit right with me there. I couldn't imagine a mutilated body floating in the sea for days on end whilst random fish happened upon it and pecked away at it. It would take weeks for it to be completely gone.

I shook my head. "No. I've seen umpteen murder documentaries about bodies disposed of at sea. Even taking into account decomposition and other factors like rough seas and sea birds picking at it, you're looking at a minimum of two weeks before it's nothing but bones. That's two weeks of possible ships going past and sighting it, no control over where the current takes it, it's too high risk."

He gave a light chuckle. "You're either too obsessed with murder documentaries or too clever for your own good."

I grinned. "My vote is both."

He laughed. "I'm inclined to agree."

"Are you going to tell me what really happens to the bodies?"

He pulled his lips into a thin line and sighed. "Sirens have what you might call pets."

"Pets. You mean like tuna? Or maybe a seahorse?"

He tipped his head back and laughed. "Not quite. More like giant squid."

My jaw dropped. "They're an actual thing?"

"I'm afraid so. Whatever the sirens don't eat they give to their squid."

"Well, I guess that explains the food source for giant sea monsters."

Marcus laughed. "Like I said, nothing gets wasted."

"Clearly," I replied, raising an eyebrow. "If they come on land to find their…meals, how does that work with having to live in the water?"

"Their water dwelling times are dictated by the moon. On a full moon they need to be in the sea for the duration of it. The other phases, as the moon becomes more of a crescent, they get more time on land. I don't know the full ins and outs of it."

"That's quite cool. Speaking of the full moon—"

Marcus' phone rang, cutting through the conversation. He took it out of his pocket, glanced at the screen, and sighed.

"Gordon."

My heart dropped like a stone through water. I couldn't hear what exactly he was saying and Marcus' poker face gave nothing away either.

"I'm not sure that's a good idea," Marcus said. "I

think you've done enough damage."

Then after a pause, "You've never wanted to apologise in your life. What are you after you slimy weasel?"

Marcus glanced at me and then said, "I will ask her and let you know."

With that, he ended the call.

"It would seem that Gordon wishes to apologise to you in person, for upsetting you last night."

I raised my eyebrows. "Oh. Ok."

Marcus shook his head. "Don't fall for it, Caitlyn. He's a rotten toad who does absolutely nothing without a reason. He's up to something."

"It's an apology," I said, shrugging my shoulders. "What harm can an apology do?"

He snorted. "With him, a lot. It won't just be an apology. That man has never apologised for anything in his entire miserable existence. He's a scheming, narcissistic, manipulative b—"

"I get it," I said, smirking. "You don't like him."

"No, you're right. I absolutely despise him. He's a wretched creature that should have been killed at birth. Or better yet, not even conceived."

I rolled my eyes. "Marcus, he's your family."

"Just because I'm tied to him by blood, doesn't mean I have to like him."

I thought about that for a moment. "That's a fair point. I'll give you that."

"You're not going to accept, surely?"

I shrugged my shoulders. "Why not?"

Marcus raised an eyebrow. "Well because of all the reasons I just gave."

I laughed. "They're your opinions on his personality. Not reasons as to why I shouldn't accept an apology."

"Those reasons are your reasons."

"I think the least he could do is squirm as he says sorry to my face for all the trouble he's caused."

He scrubbed a hand over his face. "Ok, fine, if that's what you want, so it shall be."

"Oh, stop sounding so doom and gloom. He'll come over, say sorry, and that's that. It'll be all of a two-minute chat."

"Whoa," he said, lifting his hands. "What do you mean 'he'll come over'?"

"If he wants to apologise to my face, Marcus, he needs to come round."

He shook his head. "No way. I'm not having him know where you live."

"Do you really think he doesn't know that already?"

"That's not the point."

"It's not like I'm going to invite him in. He can stand outside and say it."

"Born vampires don't need invitations into places, Caitlyn."

A spear of fright lodged itself in my heart. "I didn't know that…"

"Are you going to listen to me now?"

"I still want him to say sorry to my face."

Marcus sighed. "Fine. Then we can meet at mine. I'll sort it out with him."

"Thank you," I said. "My bubbles are shrinking; I think it's time for you to leave."

He chuckled, leaned down and pecked my lips, then left the room.

I pondered over the situation with Gordon. When I thought back to how smug and sly he'd been when he spoke to me, enjoying the little riddles he spoke in, I realised that what Marcus said about him was more than likely true.

Realistically though, what harm could accepting an apology do?

CHAPTER EIGHT

By the time I emerged from my bath, my skin had wrinkled like an old plum and to my utter disappointment, Marcus had put his shirt back on.

"Hang on a minute," I said, walking over to the bed. "How come you get to see me in nothing but a towel, yet you're fully dressed? There's something awfully one sided about this."

He grinned. "You didn't say that our agreement reached beyond the bathroom."

I rolled my eyes and tutted. "Stop being so pedantic and get your shirt off."

Chuckling to himself, he obliged. I couldn't take my eyes off his body. Something about it seemed so…unreal. Then again, his very nature had been nothing but a fantasy to me several days ago.

"Having a good look?"

His cheeky voice dragged me back to reality. My

cheeks immediately flushed with heat and I turned away to my wardrobe to dig out my pyjamas.

"You don't have to point out my staring, you know," I said, giggling. "Just enjoy it and be quiet. Like a live model in an art class."

He laughed. "Your wish is my command."

I pulled out a black and white spotty vest top and a pair of lilac pyjama bottoms. On autopilot, I undid my towel, then realised who was sitting on the bed behind me. Luckily, I had my back to him or he'd have gotten a good flash of my front.

"You don't have to be shy," he said, his voice suddenly soft and tender.

I turned around, my towel firmly replaced, and blushed. "But it's just…awkward."

He slid off the bed and walked over to me. "I've seen you in some stunning underwear. You laid on my bed and revelled in my touch. You weren't shy then."

I wanted to hide my face in my hands. "That was different."

"How was it different?"

My heart pounded against my ribs. My entire body seemed to heat up ten degrees as the memory of that night flooded my mind. "We were…you know…in the heat of the moment and all that."

He closed the gap between us, his sapphire eyes firmly locked onto mine, and brushed my cheek with the back of his hand. "What if we create a moment now?"

My breath hitched in my throat. This man had a way of changing my entire emotions in a split second. Curiosity crept in, making me tempted to drop my towel and see his reaction. A very small part of me still screamed for decency though and kept the towel firmly done up.

He leaned in and pressed his lips to my left cheek. I held my breath and closed my eyes. He kissed me again but this time lower. I shivered. His next kiss hit my jawline and he touched a hand to my right shoulder, grazing his fingertips across my skin.

Goosebumps sprang up out of nowhere, taking my sensitivity sky high. He kissed me again, this time on my neck. An excited quiver took control of my muscles and I stood there absolutely helpless and lost to this incredible man in front of me.

He brought his lips to my ear and whispered, "Are you feeling in the moment?"

I licked my lips and nodded, still keeping my eyes shut.

He pressed his lips to my ear, and I gasped. He put both hands on me, running his fingers with a feather light touch over my collarbone, around the base of my neck, down my arms. All the time, he hovered near my ear with his mouth, his warm breath skimming across my skin, sending tremble after tremble through my body.

As he trailed his fingers down to the knot in the front of my towel, I leaned my head back against the wardrobe and found myself willing him to take the towel off. He pulled at the knot, releasing it from my body. I stood there fully naked, eyes closed, in front of Marcus, and the only thing I felt was power.

I opened my eyes and met his, almost gasping at the lust and desire blazing through them. After a couple of seconds, he broke our eye contact and inched his burning gaze down my body. The further south he travelled, the quicker my breathing became. I remembered that night in his room minute by minute, the feel of his hands on my body, and how fantastic it felt.

Before I'd even thought it through, the words escaped my lips. "Touch me."

He flickered his eyes back up to mine in an instant. He reached out and skimmed his fingers around the base of my neck. The feather light touch sent a violent shudder down my spine. As he trailed his fingers towards my cleavage, I squeezed my eyes shut.

"Caitlyn," he whispered.

"What?" I whispered back.

"Look at me."

My heart somersaulted as I opened my eyes. I met his sapphire depths and found myself all but hypnotised. For the briefest of moments, I wondered if this was what being compelled felt like. I couldn't have torn my attention from him to save my life.

As he moved his fingers between my breasts, I found myself willing him to go lower. He kept his eyes on mine, slowly tracing his fingers down my stomach. When he passed my belly button, I bit my lip and held my breath.

"Just relax," he said, his voice so soft and gentle.

I let my breath out but couldn't ignore the pounding of my heart against my ribcage. It almost hurt. I expected him to go straight down south but when he veered off to one side and grazed the top of my left thigh, I almost let out a sigh of relief.

He closed the gap between us and with his free hand, slid it around the back of my neck, pulling me in to him. Before I could even blink, his mouth covered mine, his tongue parting my lips with intense hunger. I curled my arms around his shoulders and pressed myself against him. His warmth made me want to be as close to him as possible. The feel of his hard muscles pushed against my soft skin sent my mind crazy.

So focused on thinking about his enticing body and the heat radiating from him, I completely forgot about his hand still being on my thigh until he moved it between my legs. I gasped and moaned into his mouth. My entire body seemed to come alive with excitement.

Just as he slipped a finger lower, between the folds of my skin, a loud banging came from my apartment door. I jumped away from him like a naughty child who'd been caught doing something she shouldn't have been.

Marcus sighed, put his shirt back on in a flash, and stomped up towards the door. I bent down and grabbed my towel, rewrapped myself, and opened the wardrobe door, hiding myself from whoever had the world's worst timing.

"Joanna," Marcus said, the surprise in his voice hard to ignore.

"Cat?" she called.

I popped my head out from behind the open door and smiled, hoping there were no indications of what had just happened. "Hi. You ok?"

The edges of her mouth looked like they were tugging into somewhat of an amused smile. "Your dad is asking for you."

"Oh!" I said, my entire face erupting with heat. "I've just got out of the bath. Let me get my pyjamas on and I'll be right there."

"Ok," she said, her eyes twinkling with amusement. "He's sat up in bed drinking tea."

She turned and walked back out, her and Marcus exchanging a momentary glance as he held the door open for her. I felt like smacking myself in the face. How could I be in here doing things like *that*, when my dad sat mere metres away asking for me?

I snatched at my pyjama top and mentally cursed myself. I really was the epitome of a bad daughter. No, a bad person.

"Are you ok?" Marcus said, coming back to me. He reached out and touched a hand to my shoulder, but I shrugged him off. "Caitlyn?"

"No," I replied, not even looking at him. I pulled my pyjama bottoms on and stood up straight as I pulled my hair back into a ponytail. "What kind of a person does things like that when their dad is feet away, dying?"

"I think you're taking this out of proportion," he replied. "It's a part of life. Are you supposed to put a hold on everything you enjoy because of the situation?"

For some reason, his words struck a chord, an angry chord. I spun around and glared at him. "That 'situation' is my dad, Marcus. And it's hardly right that I'm in here getting felt up by you when he's in there asking for me."

"You weren't to know though, Caitlyn. You're not psychic."

"That doesn't make it any better. You think Joanna couldn't tell something had gone on? This is so embarrassing."

"Being intimate with your boyfriend isn't embarrassing, Caitlyn. It's natural."

I rolled my eyes and all but spat out my next words. "Stop making this about you. This is about anything but you."

He reached out and grabbed my wrist, stilling me

for a moment. "Actually, I'm making this about *you*. You have a life, Caitlyn. You have me. You have friends. Are you supposed to put all of that on hold and not have fun because your dad might want you at any given moment of the day?"

"I…"

"If you'd been out shopping with Hannah and Joanna had called, would you have felt like this?"

I thought about it for a moment. "Well, no."

"So what makes going out shopping any different to this?"

"Because it's seedy."

As soon as the words left my mouth, I wanted to rake them back in. It was just an instant response that clearly hit home. Marcus let go of my wrist and backed up a couple of steps. His eyes, moments ago full of passion and lust for me, were now filled with disappointment.

"Go and see your dad," he said, sitting back down on the bed. "I'll wait here."

I forced this current problem to the back of my mind and ran into the house. As I approached Dad's bedroom door, I could hear him chatting with Joanna about Midsummer Murders—one of his all-time favourite TV shows. He sounded happy and back to his normal self.

"Hey, Dad," I said, shuffling from foot to foot in the doorway.

"Pumpkin," he said, patting the empty space on the bed beside him. "Come here. Have a chat with your old dad."

He looked…frail, old, weary. He didn't look his young sixty-five, he looked like an old eighty at least. The bags under his eyes and the amount of weight he'd lost stood out like a sore thumb. How could I not have noticed he was in such a state before?

I glanced at Joanna who flashed me a smile and stood up to leave. "I'm going to get back to the twins. Guessing my neighbour is pulling her hair out by now. I'll see you in the morning."

"Thanks, Joanna," Dad said.

"Thank you," I said to her, giving her the warmest smile I could muster.

She left the room, leaving an awkward silence behind.

"I think I owe you an apology," Dad said. "Sit down."

I sat down next to him and he reached out and grabbed my left hand. That one single gesture had tears welling up inside me in an instant.

"I'm terribly sorry, Cat. I really don't know how to express how sorry I am," he said, his eyes watering. "I thought I was protecting you, well everyone really, but especially you, by keeping the truth to myself. I realise now what a terrible mistake that was and I really am sorry."

"Protect me from what though?"

"The way I saw it, the less time you had to live with me being like this, the better. I could deal with a drawn-out death, but I didn't want to put you through that. I…" his voice cracked "…I love you too much to do that."

"Oh, Daddy," I said, bursting into tears and flinging my arms around him. "I love you."

He wrapped his arms around me and squeezed me tight but it was nothing like the hugs he used to give; it felt weak and barely there yet I knew he was giving it his all. That broke my heart even more.

"I promise I'll behave now. You can run around and nurse me as much as you like."

I pulled back and eyed him with suspicion. "That's a sudden turn around."

"I'm tired, Caitlyn. I get up and get dressed and I need a sleep just from doing that. Trying to pretend everything is normal has completely exhausted me. This fall today has made me realise it's time to take a step back. I need to get you up to speed on the books, so I want you in here every morning. Ok?"

I nodded.

"Now," he said, grinning. "Tell me about your weekend."

I took a deep breath and spent the next fifteen minutes detailing Dad on every aspect of my weekend. By the time I'd finished, I felt rather tired. How had I gone through all of that in a weekend and thought nothing of it?

Dad smirked. "So you're talking to him again now?"

"Only because Luke rang him to come here. Otherwise he'd still be in the doghouse."

Dad chuckled. "You're so stubborn and bloody minded, just like your mum."

I grinned. "Would you rather I was spineless and let things go?"

"Not at all. At least I know you can stand up for yourself."

"Do you think he was telling the truth?"

He pulled his lips into a thin line and sighed. "Yes, I do. Marcus is a stand-up, honest guy. He can give you things I could only ever dream of. He has no reason to lie."

"Of course he does," I shot back. "Not wanting

me mad at him for one."

"From what I know of him, he would admit to something and make amends for it if he was in the wrong. He thinks the world of you, Caitlyn. Don't let some silly argument get in the way of what could be the best thing to ever happen to you."

I giggled. "Are you sure you don't want to date him, Dad?"

He chuckled. "Like I explained when you first came here, I want you to have a solid guy by your side who will look after you when I'm gone. I know you will have that in Marcus."

"He let me wear his ex's dress. In front of all his family. Do you have any idea how embarrassing that was?"

Dad pursed his lips. "Ok, say he'd told you it was her dress. Would you have still worn it?"

I automatically replied, "No."

"Cat, if I know you, it's that you hate being upstaged. If he'd told you that was his ex's dress, you'd have done your damnedest to make sure you looked better in it than she ever did. Am I wrong?"

I couldn't help but smirk. "You might have a point."

"So really, the issue isn't that it was her dress. The issue is he didn't tell you, which by all accounts, I can wholly see why. You were excited, looking forward to this amazing dance he was taking you to with all his family. You put on this stunning dress and no doubt looked incredible. Why would he then risk popping your bubble by telling you who it actually once belonged to? It would be as dangerous as answering 'yes' to the infamous 'does my bum look big in this?' question. He was protecting your feelings and making sure you had a good night. If that cousin of his hadn't turned up, you'd have never known any different, would you? And really what harm would that have done?"

Seeing it from another perspective suddenly put a whole new spin on things. I felt bad, really bad, that I'd dragged it out for so long. In one short five-minute conversation with my dad, he'd turned things a complete one-eighty in my head. What an idiot I was. And I'd only made things worse by spending the night at Luke's.

"I've been a bit mean, haven't I?"

"Not mean, pumpkin, no. You just reacted based on how you felt. It's only human. Don't beat yourself up."

Only human. No wonder some vampires seemed to have no regard for human life. We were emotionally fragile beings at best.

"Thanks, Dad. I wish I could have spoken to you before."

He squeezed my hand and smiled. "Better late than never."

I smiled and tried my best to fight back the wave of tears threatening to rise. Would he be here next week? Next month? My heart skipped a beat then as I realised that this time next year, he wouldn't be here. I sucked in a deep breath and tried my best not to let the panic show.

"Come here," he said, patting the empty space next to him. "Midsummer Murders is about to start."

I couldn't help but smile. Carefully climbing onto the bed next to him, I settled against his side like a child.

"Live for the moment, pumpkin," Dad said,

patting the top of my head. "Don't think about the future."

I nodded and decided right then and there that I would do exactly as Dad said—live for the moment.

CHAPTER NINE

Over the next few days, my routine became one of sitting with Dad in the mornings as he showed me how to do the books and keep everything as easy as possible for his accountant to do his job. Then I'd spend the afternoons helping to finish off the rooms. Sophie would cook tea which we'd eat side by side on his bed, then we'd watch two or three episodes from his Midsummer Murders box set before falling asleep.

Joanna had become quite chatty and I wondered if this was her attempt for us to be friends. To be honest, having a friend up here wouldn't be a bad thing. I missed Hannah, my mum, and everything back down in Dorset a lot. Hannah had been bugging me to come up for a shopping trip but I didn't want to leave Dad's side for any longer than necessary, despite him telling me he had no problem with it.

Marcus stayed in my apartment most of the time.

I had no idea how he hadn't gone mad but with his 'abilities' he could hear anything within about a mile radius. Spooky but cool. I tried to convince him that I'd be fine and he didn't need to babysit me but he wouldn't have it.

He came to me one afternoon as I finished up hoovering on the top floor. I immediately thought something must be wrong. He'd turned himself into something of a hermit staying in my apartment almost exclusively.

"Is something wrong?" I asked, trying to ignore my heart suddenly leaping into a faster rhythm.

"Not at all," he said, giving me a warm smile.

I narrowed my eyes at him. "Marcus, you've barely come out of my apartment this last week and now you're suddenly coming up here to what, watch me hoover?"

He pulled his lips into a thin line and sighed. "Gordon is getting a little impatient."

I resisted the urge to facepalm myself. I'd forgotten all about him wanting to give me an apology face to face. "I forgot about him," I said, trying to stop the smirk that wanted to pop up out of nowhere.

Marcus grinned. "He's easy to forget about."

I giggled. "Well, I've finished up here earlier than I thought. Is he free now?" I looked at my watch. "I've got a couple of hours before tea."

He walked up to me and put his hands on my shoulders, looking me square in the eye. "Are you sure you really want to do this?"

"All I've got to do is listen to him say he's sorry and then it's done with. Right?"

"It's never that simple with Gordon. He's a scheming, slimy toad."

I rolled my eyes. "Marcus, your history with him shouldn't influence my decisions. What happened between you two is your business, not mine. This is exactly like the whole thing with you and Luke. I'm going to make up my own mind about people based on how they treat me."

"I understand that, Caitlyn, but that doesn't stop me from wanting to protect you from the inevitable. Luke will betray your trust and Gordon is up to something." He leaned down and pressed a kiss to my lips. As he pulled away, his eyes twinkled with mischief. "Just promise me I can say I told you so when it all goes wrong."

I laughed. "But it won't go wrong so you've no reason to get too excited about saying it."

He sighed. "Ok, Miss Snaps. Let me make a call."

Marcus called his delightful cousin as I tidied away all the cleaning equipment. I couldn't help but think over what he said. However, I stuck to my guns—until someone did me wrong, I wouldn't judge them based on their history with someone else.

"He's heading over to mine now," Marcus said, taking my hand in his. "Are you ready?"

I smirked. "Do you mean 'ready' as in acceptably dressed or ready for Gordon?"

"I'm going to refrain from answering that," he said, kissing my forehead.

Before we left, I popped my head in Dad's room. Soft snores filled the air as he laid flat out on his back. He had lost even more weight this last week, despite eating more regularly. He'd become almost nothing but a skeleton. His skin had become loose and saggy and it pained me to see him looking so ill. With his mouth wide open and his skin still a sickly shade of grey, a chill ran down my spine. He looked…dead. If it hadn't been for his snoring, I would have gone to check his pulse.

I closed the door and sucked in a deep breath. "How much longer has he got?" I whispered.

Marcus lifted my hand to his mouth and kissed the back of it. "Days."

My breath hitched in my throat. I fought back the wall of tears threatening to rise and walked outside to Marcus' car.

"Are you ok?" he said, opening the car door for me.

I nodded and took a shaky breath. "I'll be fine."

After I sat down, he closed the door and came around to the drivers side, seating himself in utter silence. I felt like I'd said or done something wrong even though I knew I hadn't.

When we hit the main road, Marcus said, "I'm sorry," as he reached over and took my hand in his.

"For what?"

"For what's happening with your dad."

I smiled and patted his hand. "It's ok. It's not like it's your fault."

He squeezed my hand and then returned his to the steering wheel. I stared out of the window, my mind blank, enjoying the beautiful views. I suddenly remembered out of nowhere that I hadn't replied to my mum's text this morning. I'd been so busy with Dad, I read it, told myself to reply later, and forgot.

I dug around in my pockets, trying to ignore my rising panic as the realisation I'd potentially lost my phone hit me.

"What's wrong?" Marcus said, pulling into his driveway.

"I've lost my phone. I need to text my mum back.

What if Dad needs me?"

"Calm down," he said, bringing the car to a stop and switching off the engine. "I'm sure you've left it in one of the rooms somewhere. It'll still be there when we get back."

I raised an eyebrow at him. "You know people. Who's going to happily hand over a brand-new phone?"

He grinned. "Ok, point taken. I'll go back and fetch it."

"Thank you."

As Marcus helped me out of the car, I spotted a bright red sports car parked at the other end of his driveway. It looked awfully expensive but also rather old.

"Gordon likes to be rather ostentatious. He has to have people admiring him constantly."

"What is it? I've never seen anything like it."

"It's an AC Cobra. Terribly expensive, rather rare, and should be painted blue."

His tone of voice gave me the feeling that he really didn't care for Gordon's taste in colour on old cars.

"Each to their own, Marcus. We can't all be the same or it'd be a dull world."

"Wouldn't be any less dull without him in it," he said, muttering under his breath.

I smirked. "Stop it and play nicely."

With a deep frown creasing his forehead, he led me to the house and into the living room. Gordon had sprawled himself all over the sofa, his long legs stretched across the corner. He propped his head up on his hands and sighed when we walked in.

"Clearly the Cobra is still faster than your Italian rubbish."

"I didn't realise we were in a race," Marcus said. He walked up to his cousin's feet, grabbed them, and then threw them off the sofa with such force, I swear I heard a bone snap. "Sit up properly. You're making the place look untidy."

A lazy smile unfolded over Gordon's face. "You know, nothing in life gives me more pleasure than seeing my dear cousin show some emotion. It's been a while, hasn't it? Say around three hundred years."

"Right," Marcus said, his voice suddenly deep and booming. It actually made me jump. "Get out. Now."

Gordon laughed and held his hands up in a surrender sign. "I'm only messing. Although I do have to say, Caitlyn wore the dress so much better."

Marcus had his hand around his cousin's throat in an instant. I didn't even see him move.

"Marcus, no!" I yelled.

His entire body seemed to be quivering. I couldn't see his face but I could take a guess the expression wouldn't be particularly friendly. Gordon didn't seem phased though. He still wore his stupid grin.

"Don't react to him, Marcus. This is exactly what he wants."

"You should listen to your little pet there, Marcus."

With a mere flick of his wrist, Marcus flung Gordon back on the sofa.

"Could you go and fetch my phone please?" I asked, putting my hand on Marcus' back.

"I am not leaving you alone with this piece of s—"

"Marcus, I'll be fine. It'll take you, what, ten minutes?"

He visibly relaxed as he became more engaged in

our conversation and turned around to face me. "Not if I go as the crow flies. More like two."

"And what can he do in two minutes?"

Marcus turned around and glared at his cousin. "You touch one hair on her head and I'll decapitate you with my bare hands."

Gordon sat on his hands. "I'll be as good as gold. Scouts honour."

"You were never in the Scouts."

"No, but I ate the leader so that's kinda the same thing, right?"

A low growl rumbled from Marcus.

"Don't," I whispered to Marcus. "Don't react."

"I will be two minutes." He leaned down and pressed a kiss to my lips. "If he does anything, stab him in the eye. Takes us a while to heal from that."

I didn't know whether to laugh or be worried. Before I could reply, he'd gone, the draft he left behind moving my hair.

"Isn't this nice? Just me and you, all alone for two whole minutes." He turned his wrist and looked at his fancy silver watch. "Let's time him, shall we?" He pressed a button, making the watch beep, then stood up grinning. "I'm saying he's going to be three minutes at least. What do you say?"

"I think you should be apologising to me, which is what you wanted to do, remember?"

"Ah, yes. My dear dear Caitlyn, please do accept my most sincere apologies for what happened at the ball. I am truly very sorry."

His dark eyes were gleaming with anything but sincerity. The smug smirk tugging at his lips told me that whatever this was, Marcus had been right. I tried to ignore the dread churning around in my stomach.

"What are you doing?" I asked, narrowing my eyes at him. "You're not sorry at all."

"The only thing I'm feeling sorry for is you, Caitlyn," he said, taking a few steps towards me.

I frowned. "You feel sorry for me? I find that hard to believe."

"What he did to you at the ball, letting you wear his ex's dress, it was rather cruel."

I folded my arms over my chest and glared at him. "We've moved on from that, Gordon."

"I'm guessing he finally fessed up to his history with Tatiana, did he then?" he said, now circling me like a shark.

I nodded. "He told me everything and I'm still here. Whatever plan you had didn't work, Gordon. Just go home and leave us alone."

He grinned at me, baring his teeth like a wolf. "I had no plan when I came here, dear Caitlyn. So suspicious. Still, it's only natural for your kind. It's in your DNA to be suspicious of those who can drain you dry for their own gain."

Rolling my eyes, I said, "It doesn't bother me, what you have to…eat to survive. It's no different to a lion needing to a savage a gazelle. It's cruel but that's Mother Nature for you." I shrugged my shoulders. "So try again."

He narrowed his eyes and cocked his head to one side. "He hasn't told you, has he?"

I tried to ignore the instant ball of fear that lodged itself in my throat. My stomach flipped over, churning with nerves. "Told me what?"

"The real reason he's leading you on, keeping you close, playing this little pretend game of love."

I should have known Gordon had more cards to

play, that it didn't just end with Tatiana. Marcus had a past; I knew that. The fact Gordon had more things to divulge crippled me with pain. It killed me that Marcus had more secrets he'd kept from me. Why couldn't he just be honest with me?

"What now?" I whispered, trying to keep the despair from my voice.

"Tell me," he said, smirking. "Have you ever thought about someone that you've not had contact with for a long time, then suddenly you hear from them in some way?"

I frowned. "Yes. And?"

"Don't you find that a little odd?"

I shrugged my shoulders. "It's just coincidence."

"Is it? What about…I don't know…say we've had a heatwave and you're secretly wishing for a thunderstorm. Does one happen that day or the next?"

My mouth started running a little dry. "Coincidence."

"Ever fancied watching an old film and it then just happens to be on TV? Ever needed a little boost of cash and something pops through the post like a tax rebate?"

"Coinci—"

"How many incidents can you attribute to coincidence before you start wondering if you're actually influencing these things happening around you?"

"I don't understand what you're saying? What are you trying to tell me?"

"You know we need blood to survive. Made vampires and born vampires can exist forever, but there is a distinct difference between the two. Did he tell you?"

"He said that vampires, when they drink the blood of a human, are passed on that human's remaining life. So if a forty year old man had another forty years to live, then the vampire gets that forty years."

"Correct," he said, nodding. "But did he tell you that's not how it works for us? For those of us who are born vampires?"

Fear pricked my heart. I knew whatever he said next would not be something I wanted to hear. "I…I presumed it worked the same way…"

"It does, kind of. You see born vampires aren't the evolutionary leap that he likes to think we are. We were born from magic, Caitlyn. It's magic that allows us to procreate, to exist, to pass on our gifts to others, either through offspring or…" he exposed his canines, flicking his tongue over their sharp points "…through other means. That magic still runs through our veins. We need it to continue living."

I stepped back, trembling. My head was whirling at a sickening speed. "Magic? What? I don't understand…"

"Witches, Caitlyn," he said, all but hissing. "Born vampires need the blood of witches to survive. Regular human blood does nothing for us. Well, I lie. It does. It makes us lethargic, slow, like humans and junk food." His eyes glazed over, no doubt with his talk about blood. He focused back on me, his black eyes gleaming once more with dark secrets. "You have that blood, the food source that sings to us like a beautiful siren."

My knees went weak. "Witches? Blood? My blood?" I tapped my chest with my index finger. "I'm not a witch."

He chuckled. "Oh, but you are, dear girl. I can

hear the magic running through your veins, it calls to me like nothing else on Earth. I know that sound, I've hunted it for nearly five hundred years." He bent down, placing his head near mine, and inhaled deeply. "That scent…ahhh…it's so sweet, so fruity, so delicious. I'm almost drooling just at the thought of tasting you."

"Do it then," I said, determined to show him he didn't scare me. "I'm not afraid of you."

A sinister smile spread over his pale face. "If only it were that simple. You see, there's a slight complication with witches and vampires. If a witch happens to fall in love with a vampire, her blood sings only for him. Should another vampire dare to…" he reached out and traced his fingertips over my neck, making me jump "…take a bite, her blood will kill them. Burn them up from the inside out like a fireball."

I faltered, not really knowing what to say. What the hell was this? I needed to sit down. My entire world was spinning at a rate of knots all around me, like a carousel out of control.

"Unless I wanted to die, which believe me, I really don't, then you, my dear Caitlyn, are utterly safe. You see, where it concerns born vampires and witches, it's really quite the case of survival of the best. Any vampire who has the heart of a witch will live for a long time."

"Because she's what, a constant food source? What about when she dies?"

"You're being very gender specific here. Witches are male, too. As for your question, well, it's quite simple, really. When the witch dies, the vampire simply moves on but sixty years of ingesting a witch's blood, all that magic, will last a thousand years at least."

"What…what if the witch doesn't fall in love with the vampire?"

He shrugged his shoulders. "Then it's just another regular meal."

I stifled a gasp. "What are you telling me? That he's just keeping me as some sort of pet, some sort of blood donor?"

"I have no idea. It may well be that he has grown fond of you but for certain, he's just ensured his own life by another thousand years, as well as guaranteeing no other vampire can feed from you."

"What if…what if I fall out of love with him?"

"It doesn't matter. Once a witch has fallen for a vampire, her blood will only ever be for that one vampire. Whether you stay with him or not, no other vampire can ever touch you for as long as you live."

I let that sink in for a moment. That meant I was protected, for life. No fangs could ever pierce my skin except for Marcus'. He knew all the lore. Had he made me fall in love with him to protect me? Or was it all for his own selfish gain, safeguarding his next thousand years if I stayed with him until I died?

"You're in love with him, Caitlyn. One sip of your blood will last him a year. That's the power that runs through your veins."

"At what cost to me?" I asked. I regretted the question as soon as the words passed my lips.

"The golden question. When a vampire feeds from someone, it's a very intimate experience. As your blood passes through our bodies, it enables us to reach your mind. We get inside your head, speak to you, show you things, create a bond…a personal connection like no other. The more we feed from you, the stronger that union becomes."

The penny dropped then. "That's why made vampires get through so many human girlfriends?"

He nodded. "Indeed. They have to cut the ties before it consumes the human completely. Three months is about the max. For us born vampires, we spend our time hunting for witches that haven't been claimed."

"Is there many?"

"Oh yes. If you know where to look. It can be quite challenging at times."

"I thought our blood sang to you 'like a beautiful siren'?"

He grinned. "Oh, it does. But we have to be within a couple of miles to hear it."

"How do you know when one has been 'claimed'?"

"Scent. If we smell another vampire on them then we know they're off limits."

"But what if they've just been fed off of?"

He shook his head. "Doesn't work like that. There's a stark difference between the kind of scent left from a brief interaction and the kind of scent left from something more. There's also a theory, although it's widely disputed amongst our kind, that the blood of a witch who is in love sings sweeter than the blood of a witch who isn't. I personally think it's true. I haven't heard blood sing like yours for a long time." He leaned down and whispered, "In my world, a long time is a *long* time."

I shivered as his breath skimmed over my neck. Despite what he'd told me, I still didn't feel any safer around him. For all I knew, there was something else he was holding back from me.

He perked his head up and stared behind him, like

something had caught his attention. "We have company." He backed away from me and stood by the bay window, gazing out over the landscaped gardens.

Seconds later, Marcus rushed in. He glanced at me, briefly, then narrowed his eyes on his cousin. His entire face hardened, dark shadows falling over his handsome features.

"Hello, cousin," Gordon said, turning around and grinning. He glanced down at his watch. "Two minutes and fifty-four seconds. I'm disappointed. When was the last time you fed?" He flickered his gaze over to me.

"What did you say to her?" Marcus said. He flew across the room in the blink of an eye and grabbed Gordon by his collar. "You snake. What did you tell her?"

"Marcus," I said, rushing towards them both. "Let him go. It's not his fault."

His knuckles strained white where he had hold of Gordon's shirt. He shoved his face right into Gordon's and said, "I should kill you for this."

Gordon flashed him a wily grin. "For what? Telling her the truth? Why you're keeping her around like a little pet?"

A low growl rumbled around the room. It seemed to almost vibrate right through me, shaking me to my core. In the blink of an eye, Gordon flew through the air. He landed against the living room door with a resounding thud. Almost instantly, he jumped back to his feet, his dark eyes glinting at the promise of a challenge.

"Stop!" I yelled, as Marcus went for him again. "Just stop it. You can't blame anyone but you, Marcus. This is on you."

He stopped, his chest and shoulders heaving as he looked at me. "And how do you figure that?"

"You lied to me. Again."

"No, Caitlyn. I was protecting you. You didn't need to know any of that. None of it makes any difference as to how I feel about you and I didn't want you to think otherwise."

"So what? You were just never going to tell me? Did you expect me to live a life half in the shadows based on what you felt I needed to know?"

He pulled his lips together into a thin line. That was all the answer I needed.

"Do you think that's fair? Don't you think I deserve to know the full depths of what I'm getting myself into?"

"My world is very complicated, Caitlyn."

"If what he said is true then it's also my world too, Marcus."

"The less you know, the better. Plausible deniability and all that."

"Really? Plausible deniability. To who? Who would I even need that for?"

Gordon started chuckling. Marcus punched him square in the face, sending him back across the room.

"Marcus! Stop it. Stop it now or I'm leaving."

With his fists clenched he turned his back on his cousin and faced me squarely. "Do you trust me?"

"I…I…what kind of a question is that to ask after finding out I've been lied to, *again?* I can't answer that, Marcus, and it's unfair of you to ask me."

A laugh came from the other side of the room. I ignored him. Gordon seemed to like nothing more than stirring up trouble, but he had been the one to fully enlighten me to my predicament.

"Don't you start," I said, turning to Gordon. "You needn't think you've scored any brownie points by creating all this. Get out." He raised an eyebrow. "Now."

"You can walk out of your own free will or I can throw you out," Marcus said, coming to my side. "You heard her. Get out."

Gordon let out a sigh and then held his hands up. "Ok, chill out. I'm leaving." He moved towards the door, flashed Marcus a beaming smile, and said, "I'll see you soon."

"If I ever see you again, I'll kill you."

Chuckling, Gordon slipped out of the door and out of our lives. Hopefully for good.

CHAPTER TEN

As the sound of Gordon's car roaring down the drive died down, I turned to Marcus and waited for him to say something. He glanced at me and then looked down at the floor like a naughty child who'd been caught out.

"Are you not even going to give me an apology?"

"I have nothing to be sorry for, Caitlyn. I felt I was doing the best thing for you."

"Oh, please. Save me the hero routine—it's starting to wear a bit thin. You'd best start talking or I'm going to start walking."

He looked up at me and smiled. "Did you mean for that to rhyme?"

I stared back at him, poker faced. "Were you planning on telling me I'm a witch?"

When he looked back down at the floor, an arrow of pain hit me right in my heart. "You're unbelievable.

What were you planning then? Just letting me live the rest of my days at your side thinking I'm a regular human?"

He scrubbed his hands over his face and sighed. "The less you know about this world, the better."

"Yeah, you said that already. Next excuse?"

"I don't want you mixed up with the witches, Caitlyn. They're not nice people. You don't belong in that world."

"Don't you think I deserve to have the choice? And just because the ones you've met aren't nice, why does that mean they're all the same?"

"You know how old I am, Caitlyn. I've yet to meet one witch who isn't all for her own gain."

"Sounds to me like you'd have plenty in common."

The pain that filtered through his eyes from my words made me want to take them back but the anger and hurt I felt at being lied to, again, overpowered any guilt I had of making him feel bad.

"I wasn't keeping this from you for my own gain."

"How were you doing anything else?"

"Anyone from my world would know what you are within an instant of meeting you. The way people were staring at you at the ball, that wasn't because you were wearing some dress that belonged to my ex, it was because of the power running through your veins."

I smirked. "And let's not forget the way my blood sings because I'm stupidly in love with you."

"Is that how you feel? Stupid for being in love with me?"

My jaw dropped. "Are you actually making this about you right now?"

"I'm sorry, I just…I'm flattered that you feel that

way for me."

The mix of nerves and disappointment in my stomach made me feel ill, but I had to ask the question. "But you don't feel that way for me?"

He came towards me and took my hands in his. "I feel a lot for you, Caitlyn. More than I've felt for anyone in a very long time." My heart started to soar and hope trickled through my veins. "But I have to be very careful. I don't want a repeat of the past."

As soon as he said 'but' my heart sank and the hope in my veins evaporated, leaving nothing but a build-up of emotions behind. I took my hands back and moved away from him.

"You should know I'm not your past, Marcus. Do you think I'm suddenly going to beg you to turn me into a vampire or something?"

"No, nothing like that. I just want to make sure this is right, that's all."

I couldn't quite think straight. My head was spinning at a hundred miles an hour. How could he suddenly be doing a complete one eighty on me? Why? I wandered over to the sofa and sat down, trying to get a grip of my new reality. An hour ago, I'd been a regular human girl with a vampire boyfriend. Now I was suddenly a witch with a vampire possible boyfriend.

"I don't understand," I said, looking up at him. A hazy film of water blurred my vision, but I didn't care, I couldn't have stopped it even if I wanted to. "You did everything you could to make sure we were 'courting' and now you're saying you don't feel like that?"

"No, not at all," he said, sitting down next to me. "I still want a future with you. I just…with everything that's happening at the moment, I don't want us to fall into some trap where we see nothing but each other and become oblivious to the world around us."

I couldn't wrap my head around this. What the hell was he doing? "Is this because I now know I'm a witch?"

"No, of course not. With Gordon hanging around and causing carnage as he usually does, I don't want to rush into anything."

"And that includes you telling me how you feel about me?"

He pressed his lips together and looked away.

"If you don't feel the same way for me as I do for you, I get that. I'm a big girl, you won't hurt my feelings."

He took a deep breath and then finally met my eyes. "If anything, it's the complete opposite."

I hadn't expected that at all. I didn't know what to say or if I even dared move. Talk about revelations. The way he'd been talking was almost as if he were trying to let me down gently and ignore the way I felt about him. Now butterflies cartwheeled through my body and optimism filled my head with endless possibilities.

Figuring he might be feeling rather nervous after that admission, I put my hands on his and smiled at him. "I think we should go back to mine. I want to check on Dad."

He nodded. "Sure." He delved into his pocket and handed me his car keys. "Can you just give me a minute?"

A little taken aback, I nodded and took them from him. As I walked outside, it suddenly dawned on me that I could take his car for a joy ride and he'd be able to do nothing about it. I grinned and wondered how fast I'd have to drive before he couldn't keep up.

Just as I clicked my seatbelt in, he emerged from the house, a pained expression haunting his handsome face. Had I just made him admit something he didn't want to?

***

The drive home would have been silent if it hadn't been for the local radio station chattering on about Brexit and the possible implications we could be facing. He parked the car up and got out, but much to my surprise, he didn't come around to my door. Something was wrong. I could feel it in my gut.

"I'm going into the house," I said. "Are you coming?"

"No," he said, shaking his head. "I'll stay in your apartment."

With that, he disappeared into my apartment. I couldn't help but wonder what the hell was going on. I wished he'd just talk to me and stop feeling like he had to protect me from every damn thing. I wasn't some delicate china doll that needed to be wrapped up in cotton wool.

As I headed into the kitchen, Joanna came through from the hallway, sweat glistening on her forehead and her cheeks flushed.

"Cat, thank God you're back. You couldn't help me with the top floor could you please? I've still got beds to change and hoovering to do."

"Of course. Let me just check on Dad."

I creaked open Dad's door to see he was still fast asleep. I couldn't help but look at the rise and fall of his chest to make sure he was still alive and breathing.

Carefully closing the door, I headed upstairs to help Joanna. My afternoon excursion had left her in somewhat of a pickle and I couldn't help but feel bad. Poor woman had enough on her plate with the twins, let alone me dumping more work on her.

"I'm so sorry," I said, as we changed one of the beds together. "Just some family drama needed taking care of."

"That's ok," she said. "Anything juicy?"

She'd been really making an effort to be my friend the last few days and I actually had become quite fond of her company. Plus, having someone to talk to wasn't an unwelcome thing at all.

"You remember the ball the other night where Marcus' cousin let slip about the dress being his ex's?"

She nodded.

"Well, he wanted to apologise to me but all he's done is caused another argument. I'm not entirely sure where me and Marcus are to be honest. He's gone very quiet and…not himself. Isn't it crazy how things can change just like that?" I clicked my fingers together and sighed.

Mentally I couldn't help but think how crazy it was that in the last hour I'd learned I was a witch, whatever the hell that meant, and that Marcus might potentially be leading me on in order to preserve his own life. I really didn't want that to be true, but his behaviour had changed so drastically in the space of a few short minutes, I didn't know what to think right now.

"Life is cruel," Joanna said, plumping one of the pillows. "I think Mother Nature likes the fact she can send someone's life into a spin in the blink of an eye."

"Quite possibly. She is rather cruel at times."

We finished the bed in silence. I fetched the hoover in as Joanna scooped up the dirty bedsheets. As I turned back around to turn the hoover on and start making my way around the room, Joanna stood in front of me, the dirty bedclothes piled up to her chin, and a curious look on her face.

"Are you ok?" I asked, becoming slightly concerned.

She nodded. "I think it's time to stop dancing around each other."

I raised an eyebrow. "What do you mean?"

"I know what he is."

I felt like I'd been sucker punched. "What are you talking about?"

She smiled in such a way that I instantly knew she was talking about Marcus. "I know he's a vampire."

I debated for several seconds as to whether to tell her she was insane or go with it. Given the spin on my world in the last hour, I opted for the latter—I needed an outlet for all this crazy. I pushed the bedroom door closed and breathed a sigh of relief.

"Oh my God, Joanna. You've no idea how nice it is to not have to keep this to myself."

She let the sheets drop to the floor. "I bet. Well, if you ever need to talk about anything, you know you have an ally in me."

I couldn't help myself. Before I knew what I was doing, I'd reached out and hugged her. "Thank you so much. Seriously, thank you."

She hugged me back, making me feel that, actually, with a friend by my side to share this with, I could get through it. "There's no need to thank me at all. I'll be glad to help. Like I said before, I don't know why we've never become friends before."

"We certainly have a common interest now."

She laughed and nodded. "More than one actually."

I frowned. "What do you mean?"

"You're not alone, Caitlyn. I can help you."

"I don't understand?"

"I'm a witch."

CHAPTER ELEVEN

I didn't know what to say. What? Had she just said that? I found myself more stunned than when she revealed she knew Marcus' secret.

"I…um…what?"

She grinned. "I know it's not what you expected but it's true. I'm a big bad witch."

"As in spells over cauldrons and frog legs under moonlight?"

"Kind of," she said, giggling. "Except I don't have boils, warts, or a broomstick. Oh, and the black cat thing?"

I frowned and cautiously replied, "Yeah…"

"Super-secret—black cats are witches."

My jaw dropped. "As in…you…" I waved my hand around looking for the right words, but I couldn't find them.

"As in we can turn into black cats. Cool, isn't it?"

This was completely surreal to me. As I struggled to take it in, I found myself nodding and agreeing with her. "Yes."

She smirked at me and cocked her head to one side. "You look a little shell shocked."

"If I'm being honest, I've had a lot of information over the past hour that has rather turned my world upside down."

Joanna retreated to the bed and patted the space next to her. "Come, sit. Talk to me."

"What about the rest of the rooms?"

"I can sort them," she said with a cheeky wink. "Come and talk to me."

In a daze, I wandered over and sat down next to her on the side of the bed. "Apparently my dad only has days to live," I said, holding my finger out as I ticked off a list. "I'm a witch. My blood 'sings like a siren' to born vampires who need the magic in my veins to stay alive. I've somehow fallen in love with a vampire who I thought felt the same but clearly doesn't." I moved onto my next hand. "I'm untouchable to other vampires, which is a good thing, but I feel rather used by Marcus. You're a witch. You know Marcus' secret. Oh, and let's not forget the whole doppelganger thing and my freaky dreams."

Joanna let out a slow breath. "You almost had to count your thumbs in that," she said, laughing.

I couldn't help but laugh with her. "I'm sorry, this is just…I think my head is going to explode."

"Let's break this down one thing at a time. Vampires aren't the only ones who can perceive a person's healthy status. Whilst they look at people like a predator and instinctively pick out the weak and vulnerable, witches look at people as fellow souls, we can sense their troubles, their sickness, their happiness. Unfortunately, I do have to agree with Marcus. Your dad doesn't have long."

I swallowed the lump in my throat and closed my eyes to fight back the tears. "If I'm some witch then why can't I sense this?"

"Whilst it's a natural gift, it's something you need to learn to tune into. Don't worry, we'll teach you everything you need to know."

"What do you mean 'we'?"

She grinned and patted my hand. "So perceptive. You're definitely a natural. It's not just me, Cat, there are a lot of us. There are two covens just in Whitby, let alone in Yorkshire or the rest of the country. We're not a minority, we're a majority."

I frowned. "Gordon said he has to hunt in the right places to find a witch to feed off of."

"Ah, you met Marcus' delightful cousin."

"You know him?"

She laughed. "Yes, unfortunately. He's somewhat of a Casanova with witches. He's got a fair-sized collection of us. He won't have to worry about his food source for at least a millennium."

My jaw dropped. "You're joking."

She shook her head. "I wish I was. He's quite the smooth talker when he wants to be. Being empaths, it doesn't take much for us witches to fall head over heels. It's only when we come out the other side that we realise it wasn't genuine."

"Not genuine? If it wasn't genuine then how can he have a claim on your blood?"

"Some clever witch figured out years ago that this whole connection between witches and vampires isn't based on being in love at all. It's based off lust."

I felt like I'd just been hit with a sledgehammer. Lust. Did this mean my feelings for Marcus weren't what I thought they were? My head started spinning at a rate of knots. Perhaps this would explain why I didn't feel more upset he hadn't said he loved me back.

"Lust?" I said, trying to get my head around it.

"Dante described lust as 'disordered love'. It's not just a sexual longing, which is what most people think it is. Lust, plain and simple, is an intense desire for something. People lust after wealth and power, some women lust after being mothers. Do you understand?"

It seemed as if blinkers had been lifted from my eyes. It made complete and utter sense. "I'm speechless."

"The witch figured out that what we crave, naturally, is an immortal life. Witches have all this magic running through their veins, yet we live like a normal human. Vampires, born from magic, live eternally. That is disorder in itself. It doesn't make sense. We associate ourselves with them because we desire to live forever and by being with one, we can live that through them."

"Oh my God. I'm guessing they don't know?"

She laughed and shook her head. "Of course not. It would damage their delicate little ego's knowing that, actually, we're not in love with them. We have a silent upper hand here. If we have to let them have a sip of our blood once every few years, it's a small price to pay. Trust me, you will know real love when you find it."

"I think my head is about to explode."

"What if I told you I was caught out by Gordon?"

I raised an eyebrow. "You fell for him?"

"He's a good-looking guy, what more can I say? I was only eighteen."

I shivered. "He's a slimy little toad. Speaking of which, Marcus' psychotic vampire ex might be coming to hunt me down. He refused to turn her, Gordon didn't, and now she will apparently kill any woman he so much as looks twice at."

Joanna grinned and said, "It's a good job you're not just any woman then."

I couldn't help but smile. "I like you."

She tipped her head back and laughed. "Don't you worry. No one is coming for you. Ok, I'll rephrase—no one will get near you, especially some low life made vampire."

"Thanks, but I think you underestimate Gordon and Marcus' ex."

Joanna leaned forwards and whispered, "I think they underestimate you."

"What do you mean? I know absolutely nothing. I didn't even know this world existed until a few weeks ago."

"Has Marcus explained anything to you about, well, anything?"

"He's told me all the vampire lore and Isis and Osiris, how they came to be, what their weaknesses are etcetera, but he's not told me a lot else."

She pursed her lips. "Ok. Do you know about witches being able to control the elements?"

I nodded. "Yes, that he did explain. He said that most witches have the ability to control a single element, mostly fire and air. He then said that only a handful of bloodlines are able to control two or more and that water and earth are really rare."

"Yes, that's right. No vampire knows, unless the witch reveals to him of course, which element or elements she or he can control."

"Ok…I'm not quite seeing where you're going with this."

"You are from one of those bloodlines, Cat. You have immense power running through your veins. I've felt it since the day I first met you."

When she said that, for some reason it finally clicked into place in my head. This meant one of my parents had to be a witch. Why had I been kept in the dark all my life? Surely, I had a right to know my heritage? They must have known I'd end up being involved in this world at some point.

"I'm not bothered about that right now," I said, waving my hand through the air as if batting it away. I didn't care about power; I cared about the truth and finding out what my parents had been keeping from me all my life. "Which of my parents is the witch?"

Joanna pressed her lips together and looked away.

"Joanna, tell me."

"I'm not supposed to say anything."

I sighed. "I'll just go and ask Dad then."

I stood up to leave but she pulled me back down. "Don't do that. You'll make everything fifty times worse."

"If I can't ask my dad, and you're not supposed to say anything, then I guess I'll have to ask my mum."

"No, you can't do that either."

"Why not?" I said, feeling rather cornered. "How else am I supposed to find anything out?"

"You weren't supposed to find anything out."

"What? Why?"

Silence followed for several seconds before she said, "Look, why don't you come with me tonight and I'll let my coven Elder explain everything to you."

"Come with you where?"

She smiled. "It's a full moon tonight. What do you think witches do on a full moon?"

CHAPTER TWELVE

When I watched Joanna clean the rooms, make the beds, and hoover with a flick of her wrist, I suddenly understood how she managed to do all of it on her own with the twins in tow. Simply put, she didn't do anything other than flick her wrist in each room. I was stunned and also rather excited that I might be able to do something similar myself one day. It felt like a whole new world had been opened up to me and I couldn't wait to delve in and enjoy it.

She told me to meet her at the Whalebone Arch at midnight. For the rest of the afternoon, I became nothing but a jittery bag of nerves. I ate tea with Dad and settled next to him on the bed for more episodes of Midsummer Murders. I wanted to ask him so bad what he thought about the paranormal and such, see if it provoked any conversation, but my better judgement won through and I decided to wait and see what this

Elder had to say.

Dad fell asleep around eight thirty, giving me three hours to kill in the meantime. I carefully extricated myself from the bed, taking pleasure in hearing his snores. I could easily be back by the time he woke up.

I headed to my apartment to find Marcus sat on the sofa watching a Discovery Channel documentary about some underground caves.

"Hey," he said, pausing it and coming to greet me. "Had a good day?"

I nodded. "I think I can guess how your day has gone."

He bent down and pressed a kiss to my lips. "Entirely better now you're here."

I smiled at him but for some reason it felt forced, not real. I couldn't stop thinking about the connection between us and if it was as fake as Joanna said. Was this real love or was it just lust, an intense desire to live forever through my immortal boyfriend?

"Are you ok?" he asked.

I nodded. "Of course. I've had a chat with Joanna today. I'm guessing you know she's a witch."

"Yes, I do."

"She's got some things to explain to me, but she wants me to meet her coven. Tonight."

He nodded. "Ok, that sounds like a good idea."

I had to chew on that for a minute. I expected him to kick up a fuss about not letting me out of his sight or anywhere near a coven of witches. "Really?"

"You need to learn about the world you're now a part of, Caitlyn. I'm a vampire. What can I teach you about being a witch?"

"Ok…I just expected more of a fight, that's all."

"Obviously I will escort you to wherever you need to be and bring you back."

I grinned. "There it is. The overprotective boyfriend. I can walk down a street you know."

"And at what time do you need to meet her?"

"Midnight."

He smirked. "No woman of mine is going to walk down any street on her own in the dark, much less at the height of the night."

I rolled my eyes. "Fine. If that's all the argument I'm going to get, I'll take it."

"Good," he replied, a mischievous smile tugging at his lips. "Now give me a kiss."

"Hold on a minute," I said, placing my hand on his chest. "When you said 'woman of mine', you know I'm not something you own, right?"

He locked his startling sapphire eyes onto mine for several seconds, uncertainty running through them. "I would never—"

I burst out laughing. "I'm joking, Marcus."

His entire face lightened and before I knew it, he grabbed me by the waist and pinned me up against the wall. He pressed his mouth on mine, fervent hunger clearly taking hold of him. His kiss was rough, urgent, demanding, and I couldn't help but respond to his evident need for me.

Even as I enjoyed his kisses and his hands wandering down the curve of my waist, I couldn't help but wonder if I was only enjoying this because I needed to feel like I could live forever. Was this my heart and soul talking or was it just a primal need based on my witch DNA?

Marcus pulled back, looking at me with worry filling his eyes. "Are you ok?"

"Yes, of course. Why wouldn't I be?"

He frowned. "You seem distracted, hesitant. Are you sure you're ok?"

I froze for a moment. "What makes you say that?"

"You, your body, you just seem like you're holding back, uncertain."

Oh my. Had my thoughts really affected me so much? Or was this his vampire senses picking up on the slightest little thing?

"I'm ok. Just a lot on my mind," I said, looking away. Technically, I wasn't lying.

He sighed and stepped back, smiling at me. "Still feel guilty about enjoying yourself when your dad is next door?"

I forced my lips into a smile and nodded. If that was what he thought, I wasn't going to tell him otherwise.

"Come on," he said, reaching out and taking my hand in his. "Let's watch some more Vampire Diaries before you go for your midnight adventure."

That caught my attention. "Really?"

"Seeing as it's you," he replied, giving me a cheeky wink.

We settled down on the sofa and put Netflix on. As I laid my head on his chest, I couldn't help but wonder if he'd chosen the sofa instead of the bed for a reason. If our kiss had ended differently, would we currently be on the bed?

"Stop thinking so much," he said, kissing the top of my head. "It's not good for you."

I nodded and fixed my eyes on the TV. As soon as the episode started, all worries of my current predicament disappeared. Halfway through the second episode of the night, my eyelids started drooping. The more I tried to fight it, the sleepier I became. After several minutes of fighting, I decided to close my stinging eyes just for a moment, just to ease their pain.

"Caitlyn," Marcus whispered, shaking my shoulder gently.

"Just one more minute. My eyes hurt."

A low chuckle sounded from his chest. "It's five to midnight. We need to go."

I jumped up. "What? How long have I been asleep?"

"Two hours, give or take."

"Oh crap," I said, scrabbling off the sofa. "I'm going to be late." I ran around the apartment, totally confused, then stopped and looked at Marcus. "What was I doing?"

He laughed. "Shoes."

"Right." I frantically looked for my shoes, becoming more and more desperate as the seconds ticked by but I couldn't find them. "Where are they?" I whined, looking at him for help.

He stood with his hand covering his mouth but the amusement in his eyes gave him away. He pointed at my feet and then burst out laughing.

I scowled at him. "I swear to God the instant I learn how to turn you into a toad, you're getting it."

"At least I could fit in the bath with you then," he said with a mischievous grin.

I narrowed my eyes. "Shut up and get me where I need to be."

"As the lady requests."

Before I knew what was happening, he picked me up and flung me over his shoulder. He moved so fast I couldn't even draw a breath to scream. Everything became a blur until the only thing I could make sense of was the wind whistling in my ears.

Seconds later, he set me down on the floor, in front of the whalebones, the view of the harbour twinkling behind it. I stumbled as I tried to find my feet and my head spun like I'd just been on a playground roundabout at top speed.

"You ok?" he asked, putting his hands on my shoulders and steadying me.

"Define 'ok'," I replied, trying to ignore the nausea swirling in my stomach. "If you mean am I alive, then yes, I'm ok. If you mean did you treat me like a sack of potatoes, then no, I'm not ok."

I could tell he wanted to laugh. He pressed his lips together so tight, I couldn't actually see them.

"It's the easiest way for me to carry someone and run fast. Next time I'll make sure you're in my arms and we're skipping through a meadow of daisies," he said, smirking.

I folded my arms over my chest. "I'm sorry, 'next time'?"

He grinned. "You've got to get back home yet."

"That will be with my own feet on the ground, thank you very much. Every step of the way, just to clarify."

Before he could respond, Joanna appeared, seemingly out of nowhere, standing in front of the whalebone arch. "Have you two quite finished?" she asked, her brown eyes dancing with amusement.

"I'll wait here for you," Marcus said, gesturing towards one of the benches edging the cliff top. "Have fun."

Nerves exploded inside me in an instant. How was this happening to me? A day ago, I knew nothing of this and now I was about to meet an entire coven of witches. I shivered as Joanna held her hand out.

"Take my hand," she said. "The first time is always disorientating."

I looked around me, curious. "Are we going flying or something?"

She laughed. "No, nothing of the sort. We leave that to their kind," she said, nodding towards Marcus.

"Flying?"

"Didn't he tell you anything?" she said, sighing. "They can turn into bats, just like the old legends. And dogs, but that's specific to only some."

I gasped. "No. So the whole Dracula scene where the black dog ran up the steps…?"

"Yep," she said, smiling. "He actually saw it. Not just fiction."

I gazed over the other side of the harbour. Under the full moon, I could just make out the famous steps, shadowed and ancient, and wondered what Bram Stoker must have thought when he saw that. Was he scared or just intrigued? Probably both based on the book that came as a result of it.

Placing my hand in Joanna's, I took a deep breath. "Ok, now what?"

She nodded towards the arch, only a few feet in front of us. "Now we walk through the doorway."

CHAPTER THIRTEEN

When she said doorway, she wasn't kidding. As we stepped under the arch, my entire body developed pins and needles. Then, like a shimmering haze on the horizon of a desert, everything changed. The harbour vanished, all the boats and still waters becoming solid land. The houses and shops disappeared, leaving nothing but open green fields. All that remained of anything familiar was St Mary's Church and the ruins of the Abbey, and of course the steps.

Behind me, the whalebone arch stood proud, but the Captain Cook statue had vanished, along with the sea front hotels.

"Where's it all gone?" I said, looking at Joanna, completely dumbfounded.

She pointed down the steps of Khyber Pass, if it was still called that in this world, and said, "We can only practice what we need to and truly be ourselves in the safety of another realm." She lifted her free hand up and gestured all around her. "This is it."

"So only witches can get in here?"

"Yep. No witch blood, no entry. The pins and needles you felt was the magic in the arch. It remembers every single witch who passes through it. Next time you come through it'll just be like stepping from one room into another."

"But aren't vampires technically witch blood?"

She grinned. "No. They're made from magic. We're human with magical abilities. Completely different."

As I looked out over this new realm from my high up vantage point, I noticed a huge bonfire down near the sea front. A single pole stood in the middle of it, the flames circling it yet not touching it. At least two dozen witches surrounded it, all joined by their hands around the outer edge of the fire. I frowned and squinted my eyes as I looked at the pole again. It looked like someone was tied to it.

"Joanna…"

She turned us away from it quickly and led us down the steps. "Yes, it is."

My heart flipped over and over like an Olympic gymnast. I knew what she was saying but I had to double check. "'Yes it is' what?"

"Yes, it is a person."

I became paralysed with fear. What? They were actually going to burn a person to death? What kind of messed up world was this?

"Cat, there are reasons we do what we do. We select our sacrifices carefully."

I wanted to throw up. Marcus had told me witches sacrifice people, but I hadn't expected to actually witness it. A cold sweat broke out all over me and I started trembling.

"I can't, Joanna. I can't go down there."

"It's fine. Just trust me. Let us explain it all to you. Please?"

I dared to look at the poor soul tied to the stake. They didn't appear to be screaming or panicking in the slightest. They simply just stood there. Or was that more to do with being restrained?

"How could there be any explanation for this?" I asked. "It's barbaric."

"I had the same reaction," she said. "I understand. Just let Keres explain things to you. Then you can go whenever you like."

I sighed. I'd gotten this far. Surely a five-minute conversation wouldn't hurt. "Ok. Show me the way."

"Thank you," she said, leading me down the steps again.

We carried on in silence. Once we reached the bottom of Khyber Pass, Joanna led me straight over the grass towards the bonfire. I'd expected this to be sand, the beach, but every inch of it was lush green grass, right up to the waters edge.

"Joanna." An older lady with white permed hair approached Joanna with her arms outstretched. They embraced, kissing each other on the cheek. Then the older woman settled her silvery eyes on me. "You must be Caitlyn, our newest addition. Come, dear, let me show you around."

I glanced at Joanna who stepped to one side and nodded. "It's ok. This is Keres. She's our High Priestess and one of our seven Elders. She will explain everything to you."

Dressed in a flowy white maxi dress, a warm

smile, and a cosy grandmother energy to her, I figured I'd give her five minutes. After all, she seemed to welcome me with open arms so far.

"I'm so glad you're here, Caitlyn," said Keres, guiding us down towards the bonfire in a leisurely walk. "I understand you may be feeling somewhat frightened and confused. That's why I thought I'd start off with the darkest side of our lives—sacrifices."

My heart pounded so hard against my chest, I felt certain I'd have bruises tomorrow. A ball of fear lodged itself in my throat whilst a wave of horror threatened to hurl itself out of me. My palms were sweaty, and somewhere in the insanity running through my mind, I half wondered if they were going to throw me in the fire.

"Do you believe in God, or Gods?" I asked, staring at the ground. I couldn't bring myself to look at the woman tied to the stake.

"Not in the sense you're thinking," Keres said, clasping her hands together in front of her legs. She looked so relaxed and at ease, as if this was nothing more than a nightly occurrence. "We're more spiritual than religious. We believe in souls, energy, the world around us, the elements. The magic running through our blood enables us to use all this beauty for ourselves whether it's for our own gain or for the greater good."

"Where does this come into it then?" I said, pointing at the bonfire.

"There are two sides to everything, Caitlyn. Good and evil, day and night, the sun and the moon. One cannot exist without the other. You can't have light without darkness. The magic in our veins doesn't come from thin air. It comes from things like this."

I shook my head. "I fail to see how burning

someone to death gives you magic."

She slid a slender arm around my shoulder. The friendly gesture felt off, too forced almost, but I let it be. "Have you ever noticed in a family how when there's a birth, not long after there's a death? Or someone will die and then shortly after, someone will discover they're pregnant."

I thought about that for a moment. "No, I can't say that I have."

"Well, it's a cycle. A cycle of life. Birth, life, death. All three follow each other perfectly. We don't sacrifice just anyone, they're witches themselves."

"Are you basically telling me that you kill your own kind to get more of your own kind?"

"In a roundabout way, yes."

Despite us being close enough to feel the heat of the six-foot flames, I shivered. "That makes no sense."

"Let me explain further. If a witch has not tapped into their magical abilities by age twenty-seven, they never will do, but that's not the end of it. The unused magic will simmer in their body, slowly seeping into every fibre of their being, and it will, within a matter of years develop into a number of things. They may go insane, they may develop tumours, cancer, diabetes, any number of ailments modern medicine tries to fix."

As soon as she said 'cancer' my heart skipped a beat, and I couldn't help but wonder if Dad was still sleeping.

"What we do is offer them a painless way out. They're not only helping themselves but also the people they were born into. When they pass on, the magic they once had is released back into the cosmos, able to be used once more for another witch."

"Recycling," I said, without thinking.

Keres nodded. "Exactly. This lady here, Cassandra, is twenty-eight. She's just been diagnosed with leukaemia. Fortunately, one of the nurses at the hospital spotted her case and explained her situation to her. Sadly, quite a high number of witches are born and never introduced to their real heritage. Almost all of them offer themselves to us. If they have children, we take care of them. Whatever debts or messes they leave behind, we deal with it. We're like a funeral package."

It seemed bizarre but it kind of made sense. "But why burn them? It's so…medieval."

She tilted her head back and cackled like a witch. The noise brought goosebumps up all over me.

"They get a choice. It's their life, so their ending. Some want a needle, some want to be shot, others stabbed, some—"

"Ok, ok, I get the idea. Who in their right mind would want to be burned though?"

"Cassandra's bloodline traces back to the witch trials in Scotland. She wanted to end her life in honour of them. In her eyes, she's done them a dishonour by not following her heritage in life, so she is repaying them in death. We have given her a potion that has numbed her nerves. She will feel no pain."

The brunette tied to the stake looked peaceful. Her eyes were closed as if she were sleeping and a soft smile curled her pink lips up slightly.

"Ladies," Keres said, letting go of me and opening her arms to her coven. "It's time."

The witches surrounding the flames walked towards them. To my absolute amazement, the fire moved away from them, almost walking itself towards Cassandra and the stake. Once it hit the straw and kindling underneath her feet, the witches backed off but kept their circle.

Cassandra opened her eyes and looked directly at Keres. "Thank you," she shouted.

She then closed her eyes again and let the hungry orange flames ravage her body. I was so stunned and so shocked, I couldn't look away. How could someone be so calm and at peace with being burned alive? I waited for the stench of burning flesh to hit my nose and make me hurl but it didn't happen.

"Why am I smelling nothing?"

"We temper the environment here. There's no weather, so no icy cold temperatures or roasting hot heatwaves. We also neutralised all unwanted smells. It helps when making spells if we can smell the ingredients in the rawest, purest form."

"I really don't know if this is for me," I said, turning my back on Cassandra's blazing body.

"I understand that. But let me explain a few things to you before you make your decision."

Keres held her arm out in front of her, beckoning for me to walk away from Cassandra. I didn't need any encouragement.

"What else do you need to explain to me?"

"Your heritage, for one. You belong with the witches, Caitlyn. Have you ever felt like you're an outsider, struggling to fit in, make friends, have people understand you?"

I nodded. "All my life."

"That's because you don't belong with humans, Caitlyn. You belong with us. We are your family, your friends, your brothers and sisters. You'll never feel like an outsider here."

As much as I was aware that she could potentially be manipulating me, I had to admit that no one so far had stared at me, not even so much as looked at me in a way to make me feel like I shouldn't be here. All I'd seen were warm smiles and nothing but unity. Even in Cassandra's death, everyone had been unified. Had that been part of what made her so calm?

"Joanna wasn't at liberty to discuss your parentage or the circumstances that have brought you back to us. I, however, am." Keres gestured towards two giant oak trees a few metres ahead of us. Between their branches, hanging by ropes, sat a wooden bench, a swing seat of sorts. "Let's sit and talk."

I frowned and glanced around me. I could have sworn we'd only been walking a couple of minutes, but Cassandra's fire was nothing but a dot on the horizon, a single firefly in the darkness.

"Both of your parents are witches, Caitlyn," Keres said, sitting on the seat and patting the empty space next to her.

I grabbed the rough rope to steady myself. "What? No. That's impossible." I sat down next to her, in a complete daze. "No. It can't be true."

Keres waved a hand through the air in front of us, a patch of another world shone through, as if we were watching a TV screen. A sandy beach, bright blue skies, and the sea, it was a beautiful picture. A young woman on her own strolled into view, a straw hat on her head and her white cardigan gently blowing in the sea breeze. She held an ice cream in her left hand, her tongue winding around and around it as her strawberry blonde hair flowed behind her like a delicate train.

My heart skipped a beat and I gasped. I knew without even seeing her face that it was my mum. This was the story of how they met. I'd always loved hearing it as a kid, it was my favourite bedtime story, especially with how Mum dramatised it.

A seagull divebombed at my mum and her ice cream, startling her. She moved it out of sight and swatted at the pesky bird with her free hand, but it wasn't deterred. It kept coming back from all angles, determined to get a bite of her afternoon treat. Seconds later, another two seagulls joined the first, all taking their turns swooping down and attempting to steal Mum's ice cream.

As Mum took her hat off and waved it at the annoying pests, a man ran into view. His long legs covered the beach metres at a time. The sunlight picked out his dark hair, making it shine like onyx. As he approached Mum, he reached out with his right hand and merely made a flicking motion with his thumb and finger. The birds instantly retreated, squawking at each other and flying off.

Mum turned around, tripped over her own feet and fell over, dropping her ice cream in the sand. Dad helped her to her feet, and from there, as they say, the rest was history.

"Pay close attention to your dad's hand," Keres said, rewinding the scene to the point where Dad outstretched his arm. "I'm going to play it frame by frame. Don't blink or you'll miss it."

I leaned in and watched Dad's hand. As Keres took it through second by second, I could see it as clear as day—as Dad touched his finger and thumb together a golf ball sized circle of air appeared at the tip of his finger. When he flicked it towards the birds, it divided into three separate balls, each one pelting each bird and turning them away from Mum.

"Wow," I whispered, leaning back. I really needed something solid behind me to support me. "I can't believe I've just seen that."

"Your father is a dual elemental witch. He can control air and earth. He's very powerful."

"This makes so much sense now," I said, her last words completely going over the top of my head. "When Mum told me the story as a child, she always said that Dad had magic gems he threw at the birds to make them go away and leave her alone."

"She wasn't too far from the truth," Keres replied, smiling.

"But if Mum is a witch too, why didn't she just save herself?"

"Because she didn't know she was a witch until she met your father. Then she discovered that she herself came from a highly regarded witch family. Unfortunately, she only had power over water. Through her bloodline, she should have been born at least a dual elemental, but for some reason, nature decided otherwise."

"Oh. Is that something you can do then, predict what elements children of witches will have?"

Keres pulled her lips into a thin line. "To a degree. We can tell if they're going to be single or dual elementals. Fire is easy to sense when the baby is still in the womb, the other three, not so much, so it's still rather a 'see what you get' when they're born."

"Do you know what I am?"

A quirky smile tugged at Keres lips. Under the moonlight, her face half shadowed, I would have almost described it as sinister. "Oh, yes. You are exceptionally unique. You have the power of all four elements. We've not had a witch with that power for nearly two centuries. You are quite the exception."

"How's that?"

"The way our bloodlines work is rather complicated. Some think it's a simple case of getting two dual elementals together and breeding them to reproduce a child that has ability over all four. That's not correct. Air is dominant over fire. Fire is dominant over water. Water is dominant over Earth. Earth is dominant over Air. It seems the way it fell with your parents meant that the only element missing was the most common—fire. Where your mother should have been a dual elemental, that skipped a generation and seemingly passed into you. Combine that with your doppelganger status and you are one nuclear bomb of a witch."

I sat in silence for several minutes, stunned, staring up at the huge full moon. What was I supposed to say to that? Apparently both my parents were witches and had kept this massive secret from me all my life. Dad's little oops with the hospital letter and the truth of his cancer suddenly seemed very trivial.

"Why haven't they told me?" I said, tears blurring over my vision.

I felt completely lost, like I'd just been thrown overboard into shark infested waters. How was I supposed to navigate these murky waters on my own?

Keres sighed. She reached over and patted my hand, then said, "Because they don't know they're witches anymore."

CHAPTER FOURTEEN

My jaw dropped. "What? How?"

Rubbing her hand over the frozen picture of my dad throwing balls of air at seagulls, Keres made the image disappear, plunging us back into nothing but moonlight.

"Power is something that is lusted after by everyone. It does not differentiate between humans, vampires, witches, or anything else that exists. When you were born, it became evident almost immediately you were, well, what you are. Your parents, instead of revelling in the joys of being new parents, found themselves backed into a corner, not knowing who to trust and viewing every single person as a potential threat. By the time you started school, things had progressed to a stage where they had to do something to protect you and themselves."

I frowned. "What did they do?"

"With the aid of a couple of Elders, they put a binding spell on you. It was designed to hide your magic. In the name of plausible deniability, they both asked to have their memories locked too."

"Locked?"

She nodded. "Memories can't be erased. They're an imprint on the brain. But what we can do is lock them away so deep, you never remember. We removed all elements of magic and witchcraft from their memories so they still had the years they'd spent together just minus a few truths."

"Mum's magic gems in her story of her and Dad turned into rocks…he threw rocks at the birds. Is that why?"

"Yes, it is."

"And when they split, why did they split?"

Keres looked at the ground and sighed. "Your father came to us on his own and asked for you and your mum to move away, somewhere far away where no one would likely find you. His main concern was keeping you and your mum safe. He asked to stay here in the hope that any interested parties would expect to find you close by."

"And now I'm back. With a vampire…man friend, or whatever the hell he is, and a witch for a friend and co-worker." I nodded. "Sounds like I'm back right in the thick of it to me."

"You've nothing to fear, Caitlyn. We're all here for you and we're behind you one hundred percent."

"I…this has been one hell of a day for me. I think I need to get some sleep."

"Of course. There is one other thing though."

"Dare I ask?"

She laughed. "Your father, before he dies, we

need to release his memories or he will become a restless spirit."

"How do we do that?"

Keres held out her hand, a small vial in the palm of her hand. A rosy pink liquid filled it with tiny sparkles, like glitter, shining throughout it. "Just add this to his cup of tea. It'll bring everything back to him."

I couldn't help but look at it with suspicion.

"Take the lid off and smell it. It's quite alright."

I reached out and took it from her. Prising off the small cap, I found myself pleasantly overwhelmed with the scent of fresh air and roses. "That smells gorgeous."

Keres nodded. "It won't hurt him in the slightest. Hopefully it'll give you two some common ground to talk about before he passes."

I replaced the cap and sighed. "Thank you."

"I do need to explain your part as a doppelganger before you go though."

I'd completely forgotten about that. I wasn't sure I could even take on any more information today. "Ok, I'm listening. Can't promise I'll remember it though."

She chuckled and patted my hand again. "You'll be just fine. We all feel nervous at the beginning. It's a whole new world."

"What's with the doppelganger thing then?"

"Doppelgangers are created when someone of either great importance or great power deviates from the path they were supposed to take."

I frowned. "That makes no sense."

"Do you believe in fate, destiny?"

"I don't know. I've never really thought about it. But if you're going down that road then you could argue it was destiny they deviated from their path in the first place and therefore created the doppelganger."

"Yes," Keres said, nodding. "That is very true. However, it doesn't really work like that. Think of it as like sending a child down a path. At the end of the path is an ice cream stand with all the flavours of ice cream they could ever want. But along the path there are other distractions such as candyfloss or chocolate. Even though you've given them the helping hand to point them in the right direction, it doesn't mean they're going to go straight there."

"But then is it destiny that those distractions are there in the first place?"

"It could be argued that way, yes. It's all about perceptions really. Destiny isn't a straight line that leads you straight to what you want. It's a mere suggestion towards what you want. If you don't follow it then things will naturally adjust otherwise."

"And that's when doppelgangers are born?"

"Not immediately, but at some point down the line, yes."

I looked Keres square in the eye and asked, "You know exactly who I'm a doppelganger of, don't you?"

She didn't falter in the slightest. "Yes, I do. I knew Mirabelle very well."

It took a few seconds for things to click into place. I gasped. "Mirabelle was the elemental witch? When you said you'd not seen a witch like me for two hundred years…you were talking about her?"

"Yes, I was."

"But she's been missing for two hundred years! How am I…how is this even possible?"

"The fact you're alive means she's alive, Caitlyn. All the factors that have come into play, the hands that destiny has dealt to bring you to life is just…extraordinary. You have a purpose and a reason for being. Mirabelle was the start of that."

"Marcus is desperate to find her. Where is she?"

Keres sighed and looked down at her hands, wringing them together. "No one knows. It's as if she just vanished into thin air. Locating spells, blood work, searching every square inch of this realm and earth, we could not find her."

"I've had dreams about her. The last one I had, Marcus' psycho ex stabbed her with gold and threw her off a cliff." I gasped. "Wait, if she's a witch then how did she give birth to a vampire, to Marcus?"

"Unfortunately for Mirabelle, she became somewhat of a hot debate in the supernatural world. Some said she should have been killed at birth, others said she was a marvel of life. Her mother was a witch, her father a vampire. Vampire DNA dominates witch DNA and therefore Mirabelle became the first-born vampire with the abilities of a witch. And not just any witch either—one who could control all four elements."

"There must be others like her though?"

Keres shook her head. "People were terrified of Mirabelle and the power she had. Even in our world. Her parents never stayed in one place too long in fear of their lives. After several years of being moved around, Mirabelle had enough and stood up to her tormentors. Her mild temper tantrum caused one of the deadliest earthquakes in history. At that point, it became law that species shall not cross breed. The resulting offspring were too unpredictable and presented too much risk of exposure to the humans."

"Mild temper tantrum?"

"Yes. She didn't even try to do anything. They were in Syria, Aleppo, to be exact, in the eleventh century. Her actions killed nearly a quarter of a million people."

My hands flew to my mouth in shock. After a couple of seconds, I lowered them and said, "And you're saying I have this power?"

"No. You have more. You're a doppelganger."

I started trembling from head to foot. How was I supposed to deal with such a responsibility? I never asked for this, never even wanted it, yet somehow I now felt responsible for every person's life within a hundred mile radius.

"You say you've had dreams about her?" Keres asked.

I nodded. "Only a couple."

"That's good. It means you're connecting." She clasped her hands together and held them in front of her chest. Her eyes sparkled with joy. "My goodness, if you're connecting whilst your magic is bound, imagine what can happen when we unbind you."

"Whoa, whoa, whoa. Hold on a minute. Nobody is unbinding anything just yet."

"Don't you want to see what you can do? Don't you want to be who you're meant to be?"

I held back the smirk that wanted to form and replied, "Maybe destiny wants me to stay this way."

"Destiny brought you to us. I would suggest otherwise."

I let out a long breath and stood up. "I need some time to process this."

"Of course," she said, standing up. "Completely understandable. Although forgive me for asking, but would you not want to help Marcus?"

Her question pricked a bubble of irritation inside me. I couldn't help the words that left my mouth next. "Don't try emotional blackmail with me because it won't work. Marcus hasn't had his mum for two hundred years. I've known about all of this for less than twelve hours. I think he can wait another day or two and potentially keep thousands of people alive by doing so."

Keres looked at me and raised an eyebrow. A sly smirk tugged at her lips. "Perhaps Rosemary's little discovery all those years ago is in fact true."

"Excuse me?"

"The connection between witch and vampire being lust based." She gestured for us to walk towards Khyber Pass. "If you felt any sort of love for him, you wouldn't be putting yourself and others before him."

"Are you saying I should be helping him?"

"Oh no, dear. I'm not saying you should or shouldn't be doing anything. I'm merely pointing out that maybe you're not in love with him like you may think you are. Love knows no bounds."

Did she have a point? Joanna had put the doubt in my head earlier on, but Keres had, in a roundabout way, made me all but admit it myself. If I was so besotted with Marcus, wouldn't my first thought have been to find his mum?

CHAPTER FIFTEEN

By the time I emerged through the whalebone arch, I had no energy left. Every single fibre in me felt like lead, I ached, my head hurt, and I wanted more than nothing to just collapse in bed and forget about all of this crazy.

How had this suddenly become my life?

"Hey," Marcus said, appearing at my side from nowhere. "Are you ok? You look exhausted."

I looked up at him, questions running through my mind as to whether I felt for him like I thought I did. "I feel absolutely drained. Can you take me home please?"

"Whatever the lady desires."

"I don't even care if you treat me like a sack of potatoes. Just get me to bed ASAP."

He chuckled as he picked me up and flung me over his shoulder. I had nothing in me to even care. I closed my eyes and tried to make my mind blank as he ran back to my apartment but all I could think of was the final conversation with Keres. This man gave me everything I wanted; looked out for me, stood by my side, was insanely gorgeous, had manners to rival any gentleman, and yet I may not be in love with him like I thought. Why? Was there something wrong with me?

What felt like seconds later, Marcus laid me down on my bed. The instant I hit the mattress I groaned in relief.

"You've no idea how good that feels," I said, pulling the duvet up to my chin.

He slid in next to me and settled an arm over me as I rolled onto my side. "Sleep well," he said, pressing a kiss to my temple.

I let out a long breath and closed my eyes, instantly falling asleep.

I found myself standing on a cliff top, staring out over the sea. I glanced around me to see nothing but rolling hills behind me and ocean blue waters in front of me. This wasn't Whitby. In fact, I had no idea where on earth I was.

"Hello again."

I jumped and screamed. I thought I was alone up here.

"I'm sorry. I didn't mean to scare you."

Turning to the deep voice, I found an athletic man stood next to me. He towered over me, but I felt no threat. His warm smile and the sincerity in his green eyes eased my nerves. His brown hair harboured specks of grey, matching his goatee.

"Who are you?" I asked.

"No one you need to fear," he said. He then made a point of putting his hands in the pockets of his jeans.

Jeans. That made me stop and think. I looked down at myself to see I was wearing my clothes from today—light coloured jeans and an emerald green vest top. Did this mean I was me here?

"*Do you know who I am?*" *I asked him, meeting his jade green eyes.*

"*Of course I do. What supernatural folk don't know who you are?*"

My heart skipped a beat. "You're…??"

He gave me a cheeky wink and then right before my eyes, in a matter of seconds, he turned into a huge black wolf. When he looked at me with bright yellow eyes, I screamed and ran backwards. This was the wolf from my dreams, the one that had terrorised me that night at the Abbey.

I tripped over and crumpled into a heap on the grass. Instinct took over and I curled up into a ball, screaming and crying, waiting for the inevitable savage bite that would end my life.

"*Caitlyn.*"

Trembling from head to toe, I dared to open an eye to find a hand in front of my face. I moved my head and opened my other eye. The man had returned to his human form, clothes intact, and offered me help to my feet. What?

"*It's ok, I'm not going to hurt you,*" *he said, wiggling his fingers. "Come on.*"

Tentatively, I put my hand in his and allowed him to pull me up. "You…you're the wolf from the Abbey…" I was still shaking, almost uncontrollably and couldn't quite think straight. "You've scarred me for life."

He chuckled and pointed to a wooden bench just behind him. "That certainly wasn't my intention. I do apologise. Let's sit and talk."

I frowned. "That wasn't there before."

"*You're observant.*"

We sat on the bench, or rather, I teetered on the edge as far away from him as I could be without sitting on the floor.

"*Where are we?*" *I asked, gazing around trying to get my*

bearings.

"That's not important. What's important is the journey you're about to undertake. Do not trust the witches. You must not trust them. Do you understand?"

I frowned. "Why? They seem to pose no risk."

"There you are. I've been looking all over for you."

A female voice as sweet as honey drifted through the air. I turned to my left to see none other than Mirabelle walking towards the wolf-man. She stood behind him, her delicate hands on his muscled shoulders.

I stood up and gasped. "Oh my. Mirabelle?"

She took one look at me and beamed a smile right back at me. "It's so good to meet you, Caitlyn."

I couldn't get my head around this. Looking at Mirabelle was like looking into a mirror. Right down to the freckles. She carried an air of grace to her that just seemed so enticing, so gentle, so calm. I found myself not wanting to leave her presence.

"You're very important to our son," the man said. "You must not leave him behind, Caitlyn. It will break him."

"He's looking for you," I said, making eye contact with Mirabelle. "He's so desperate to find you."

She nodded. "It'll happen when the time is right but until then, you must be there for him. You two are very special. You're meant to be. Now you have crossed paths, you have to stay together. When soulmates find each other, it's an incredible thing." She bent down and pressed a kiss to the man's cheek. He closed his eyes in contentment. "My life makes so much sense now I've found mine."

My heart wanted to cry for Marcus. "Does he know?"

As Mirabelle opened her mouth to answer, a gust of wind blew across the cliff top. However, it didn't feel neither cold nor warm.

Mirabelle looked up at the sky and sighed. "It's time to go."

"Wait," I said, reaching my hand out. "I've got so many questions."

Mirabelle smiled as she and her man walked away from me. "All in good time."

I startled awake to find myself sitting up in bed, hand outstretched.

"Hey, calm down," Marcus said, rubbing my back. "It was just a dream."

It took me a second to realise I was back in my bed, in reality. Then as all the details came rushing back to me, my heart cracked. This was going to break him. Did I tell him or did I not?

"It was just rather real," I said, trying to push the covers off me.

"What do you need? I'll get it."

"Water, please." Less than two seconds later, I had a glass of cold water in my hand. "Thank you."

I drank slowly as I debated how to approach the situation. I had so many questions, some which Marcus might be able to answer but I couldn't ask them without giving away the dream I'd just had.

As I set the glass down on my bedside table, I blurted out, "I saw your mum."

"When?"

"In my dream."

His eyes lit up like a Christmas tree. "Is that who you were shouting 'wait' to?"

I nodded. I reached out and took his hand. "She wasn't alone, Marcus."

He gave the biggest grin I'd ever seen. "That's fantastic. I hated to think of her being alone somewhere. Was she happy? Did she say anything to you about me?"

Rather taken aback by his happiness at his mum

not being alone, it took me a minute to gather my thoughts. "She looked…radiant. There really is something rather magical about her."

He nodded. "She's an incredible woman. My dad misses her so much."

My heart stopped for a moment. How awful. Was his dad still counting on them being together? "Marcus, are werewolves a real thing?"

He narrowed his eyes at me. "Why?"

"There was one there. He turned, right in front of me, but that's not it—he was *the* wolf, the one from the Abbey."

"You're sure?"

I nodded. "Very sure."

He sighed. "Yes, unfortunately, they are a real thing. We don't get along particularly well. Conflict between species is no different in our world than it is in yo—for the humans, well between animals. You know what I mean."

I grinned. "Forgot for a minute there, didn't you?"

He chuckled. "Did this werewolf speak to you?"

I nodded. "He apologised for the night at the Abbey, said it wasn't his intention to scare me." I frowned as I recalled what happened next. "But before he could really explain anything, your mum appeared."

His forehead creased into wrinkles. "My mother was around a werewolf and ok about that?"

I glanced away. "She was more than ok with it."

"What are you trying to tell me, Caitlyn?"

I sucked in a deep breath and closed my eyes. "She was *with* him, Marcus." I opened my eyes and squeezed his hand. "She said they were soulmates."

In an instant, he dropped my hand and got off the bed. "That's impossible," he said, pacing up and down at the side of the bed. "She herself is the whole reason that relationships between species are banned. She hates werewolves with a passion."

"I know. Keres explained everything to me about your mum. Even the witches don't know where she is. I'm telling you though, she loves this guy."

Marcus shook his head. "No. I knew it. I knew someone had taken her." He turned to me, his eyes full of anger. "It's Stockholm Syndrome, Caitlyn. Those rabid wolves have had her all this time…" He turned away from me, but I could see his whole body vibrating. He was beyond livid. "Where were they?"

"I don't know. I didn't recognise it."

He turned back around, his eyes bloodshot and his handsome face creased into fury. "Describe it to me."

One look at him sent fear coursing through my veins. "I…it…was just a cliff top."

"Where?"

"I don't know!"

"Think, Caitlyn, think!"

I burst into tears. His booming voice and terrifying looks made me want to run away and hide. Mirabelle's words echoed in my ears. *You must not leave him behind. You're meant to be.*

"I don't know…it was just a cliff top. There was nothing there. Nothing. Just hills one side and the sea the other."

Marcus let out a shout of frustration. "I'm going to kill that good for nothing beast you call a friend." He took his phone from his back pocket and started scrolling over the screen. "I told you not to trust him, didn't I? Didn't I tell you not to trust him?"

"Who are you talking about?" I said, trembling

from head to foot.

"Luke, of course."

My fear evaporated and I felt nothing but anger. How dare he drag Luke into this mess? "What the hell has Luke got to do with this?"

"He's a werewolf, Caitlyn."

Chapter Sixteen

Shellshocked wasn't the word. Luke, a werewolf? No way. It wasn't possible. Was it? It would explain the hatred the two had for each other. As Marcus blasted away down the phone at Luke, demanding to know where his mum was, all the little things started coming together. The wolf weathervane on the top of his stables, the big family, his insane strength, the size of him, the fact he never seemed to sleep.

I sat back against the headboard of my bed, dazed and confused. What a day this had been. I couldn't even bring myself to say 'Luke is a werewolf' without it sounding foreign. It didn't feel right. Why hadn't he said anything before now?

Seconds later my apartment door flew open and Luke hurled himself down the hallway at Marcus. Before I could even blink, Luke had Marcus by the throat, pinned up against the wall.

"You want to say that to my face, blood sucker?" Luke said, all but growling.

Marcus grinned at him and stuck his face right in Luke's. "Give me my mother back, mutt. I know you know where she is."

I jumped off the bed and ran over to them. Luke's knuckles were white, his entire body tensed, ready to fight. I could see all the muscles and tendons in his forearm, strained with fury. Marcus' eyes gleamed with the promise of war.

"Stop it," I said, putting my hand on Luke's arm. "Please."

Luke let out a shaky breath and after a couple of seconds, he released his grip on Marcus.

"Typical mutt, letting the woman take control. Always think with your di—"

"Marcus!" I yelled. "Enough."

Marcus turned to look at me. He still looked rather frightening but somehow it didn't bother me now. I knew Luke would flatten him if he turned on me.

"He knows where my mum is," Marcus said. "His group of wild, uncivilised, dirty mongrels took my mum."

Luke glanced at me, his brown eyes full of worry. "Cat—"

I held my hand up. "Oh, we've got some talking to do but now is not the time." I glared at Marcus. "How do you know Luke has anything to do with this?"

Marcus opened his mouth, but no words came out.

"Right," I said. "This was just an opportunity to pick a fight with the closest wolf was it?"

He looked away, staring at the floor.

"For goodness sake." I turned to Luke and said, "I'm so sorry. I had a dream about his mum and he's taken it all out of proportion."

"It's ok," he said, rubbing his hand up and down my arm. "Are you ok?"

I nodded. "It's been a day of revelations to say the least. Did you know I'm a witch?" His hand stilled and as guilt trickled into his eyes, I had my answer. "Were any of you planning on telling me? Or do I literally need to thank Gordon for that?"

"Gordon?" Luke said, turning his head to look at Marcus. "She better not mean the Gordon I think she does."

Marcus didn't say a word.

"What is the matter with you?" Luke yelled, balling his fists. "Are you trying to get her killed?"

I put my hands over my face and groaned. "Now what?" I asked, letting my hands drop. "What else do I need to cram into my overfilled brain?"

"Gordon is a hitman," Luke said, staring at Marcus. He froze for a moment and then smacked himself in the head with the palm of his hand. "Of course." He looked at me and said, "You remember that creepy old lady on the beach?"

I nodded.

"I bet you any money you like she has something to do with Gordon reappearing."

I shook my head. "How do you figure that out?"

"Because I know exactly who that was and what she wanted."

Feeling nothing but exasperated, I threw my arms up in the air. "Oh yay. You know what? I actually can't deal with this right now. I'm going back to bed. If anyone wakes me up before I want to wake up, I'll turn you into my personal slave. Oh, and this place…" I motioned around my apartment "…is Austria. If you want to fight like teenage boys, take it elsewhere."

The two men looked at each and sighed.

"I'm going nowhere," Marcus said, walking back to the bed.

Luke wandered over to the sofa and plonked himself down on it. "Neither am I."

"No one invited you to stay," Marcus said. "There's no need."

"You're here," Luke replied. "There's very much the need."

"Just go," Marcus said. "Before I make you."

"Guys!" I said. "This is Austria. No one needs an invitation to stay."

Silence finally fell and I drifted back into a very welcomed dreamless sleep.

***

When I woke the next morning, I felt calm and peaceful, like nothing dramatic had happened over the past twenty-four hours. And then like a wrecking ball, it hit me. I was a witch who may or may not be in love with a vampire, I'd spoken to said vampires mum and her new lover who happened to be the demon from my nightmares, my parents were witches who had 'locked' their own memories away and bound my magic, two of my friends were a witch and a werewolf, oh, and there was a possible hitman vampire after me too.

I wanted to roll over and go back to sleep. Sleep it all away. It'd be fine then. Suddenly, I didn't pity Sleeping Beauty, I envied her.

"Good Morning," Marcus said, putting a hand on my back. "How are you feeling?"

I sighed. "Like I don't know which way I'm being pulled."

"I'm sorry."

I turned over and looked up at him. "For what?"

"For how you're feeling."

I rolled my eyes. I threw the bedcovers back and

got out of bed. "And there was me thinking you might be saying sorry for your behaviour last night."

A light chuckle sounded from the sofa. I kicked the back of it and said, "Don't you start. You're in just as much trouble."

The chuckling abruptly stopped.

"Of course I'm sorry for last night," Marcus said. "I didn't want any of this to happen because I didn't want you feeling like this."

I wandered over to the kitchen and flicked the kettle on. After I set out my mug and put the tea bag in it, I turned around and folded my arms over my chest. "That sentence had a lot of 'I' in it. That strikes me as being some manipulative crap if I'm being honest."

Luke sniggered.

"Did you not hear what I said?" Marcus said, getting off the bed. "It was only my concern for you that kept me from telling you anything."

"Right…is that what made you keep Gordon away from me too?"

Marcus looked over at the sofa. Luke was still laying down but even from where I stood I could see the beaming grin on his face.

"He can't touch you in an official capacity," Marcus said. "He's my family and he's bound by rules that forbid him from killing you."

"Knowing Gordon, there is a way around it that will mean he can fulfil his contract."

Marcus pressed his lips together. "The witch is an Elder from another coven. She wants you, and if not you, then your blood will do."

The kettle boiled, the click of the switch almost making a point of his words. I poured the water into my mug and let the teabag stew.

"I wouldn't mind a cuppa," Luke said, finally sitting up.

I pointed at the kettle. "You know where the mugs are."

"But—"

I shook my head. "You don't get luxuries like having tea made for you when you've been lying to me for months."

He closed his mouth and frowned. He even pouted.

I turned my attention back to Marcus. "Were you just planning on never telling me?"

"I hadn't thought that far ahead."

"If you expect me to believe that then you really are an idiot," I said, turning my back on him to tend to my tea.

His phone rang then, cutting through the tension. He answered it and disappeared into the hallway to talk. I heard the sofa creak as Luke moved. I didn't need to watch him approach me; the hairs on the back of my neck stood up as he neared me. A soft shiver ran down my spine and I couldn't help but look at him.

"You ok?" he asked, keeping his voice low.

I nodded. "I want to be so mad at you right now."

He flashed me a cheeky grin. "But you can't be, can you?"

"Shut up," I said, pouring the milk into my tea. "I'll leave the milk out for you. Consider that a mere leaf from an olive branch."

As I turned away to head to the sofa with my tea, he reached out and caught my arm. "Hey," he whispered. "I'm sorry for lying to you."

I tried to ignore the leap of my heart as his skin

touched mine. I wanted nothing more than to sink into his chest and have his arms around me, but I couldn't. "Thank you," I replied, before backing away and retreating to the sofa.

Marcus came back down the hallway, his handsome face set into a grim expression. He put his phone back in his pocket and gave me a very sheepish look.

"What?" I asked, putting my tea on the coffee table.

"Whilst you were sleeping last night, I reached out to some contacts about my mum and the connection with the wolves—" he glanced at Luke "—I've got a really good lead and I need to chase it up."

I nodded. "That's great news. I'm really happy for you."

"But it means I'm leaving."

I stood up. "Leaving?"

He nodded.

"What do you mean you're leaving?" The rising panic inside me felt like lead trickling through my veins. I couldn't move or barely even think. How could he do this to me?

"I need to go and speak to some witches about how to find my mother. They know everything there is to know about doppelgangers. Between you and them, I can find her."

I was stunned. I literally had no reaction because I couldn't comprehend this situation to even formulate a reaction. What was he thinking? "But…but my dad…Marcus, you can't leave. Not now."

He came over to me, took my hands in his and lifted them both to his mouth. When he brushed a gentle kiss over the back of both, instead of welcoming the normal butterflies that flowed through me at his touch, I felt nothing.

"You know I wouldn't even think about this unless it was absolutely vital. Caitlyn, this is my chance, my one opportunity to finally find her after all these years. After your dream last night, I know she's calling for me. I need to do this."

"Go next week or next month, whenever, just not now."

He sighed and closed his eyes. He drew in a deep breath and then reopened his eyes. "These witches, Caitlyn, they're *old*. Older than even my family. Rumours are they were around in ancient times. They move from place to place, realm to realm. It's very rare that anyone ever knows where they are. I have to take this chance now or I could be waiting another two hundred years or more for another chance."

I stared at the floor. My mind and body felt nothing but numb. Part of me wanted to be angry at him, another part happy for him, but the biggest part had been filled with an unsettling emptiness I didn't know how to calm.

"I understand, Marcus, but I need you right now."

"I know you do, sweetheart, but you've got other people around you—Luke, Joanna, Sophie, Hannah, your mum. You'll be fine."

"I'll be here, Cat," Luke said. "If he needs to go then let him go."

"Don't side with him, Luke, please."

"I'm just saying, I'll be here for you."

"See?" Marcus said.

I narrowed my eyes at Marcus. "You'd normally be telling him to back off and to leave me alone but now because it suits you, you don't care. You really have reached a whole new level of low."

"You can't ask me to choose between you and my mum, Caitlyn."

My jaw dropped. His words ignited an ire in me I'd never felt before. "I beg your pardon?"

He dropped my hands, uncertainty flickering through his eyes. "I—"

"How dare you?" I said, glaring at him. "How dare you accuse me of something like that. Do you not even know me by now? I can't believe you would even think that, let alone say it!"

"Caitlyn, calm down." He glanced around, a nervous edge to his eyes. The apartment suddenly darkened and I turned to see the clouds outside had taken a dark turn, promising heavy rain. "I wasn't accusing you of anything."

"Don't take me for a fool. I heard what you said, Marcus. I'm not asking you to choose between me and your mum. I'm asking you to stay a few more days, that's all. My dad is right next door, dying. Your mum is alive and well. I need you, Marcus."

A low rumble sounded from the grey sky. "I can't," he said. "If I delay any further then I'm risking not finding them. I've wasted enough time already."

"How? You found out about them two minutes ago."

He pursed his lips and looked down at the floor. The penny dropped. "You mean this, don't you? Having this conversation with your girlfriend is wasting time." I snorted. "Well, isn't that just charming." I turned my back on him and walked across the room, shaking my head. What an absolute asshole.

"Caitlyn, I—"

Just hearing his voice sparked fury within me. I

spun around and yelled, "Get out, Marcus. Just get the hell out!"

He held his hands up in a surrender sign. His eyes flooded with fear. "Sweetheart, please. I don't want to leave on bad terms."

"Get out."

"If you need me, ring me. I'll be there, I promise."

"Sure."

He put his hands on my shoulders, staring me straight in the eyes. "I will, Caitlyn."

I looked away. I couldn't bear to be around him at the moment.

He bent down and kissed my cheek. "I'll call you later."

I rolled my eyes in response.

"Please don't make this any harder than it already is."

That annoyed me. "What about you making my life harder than it already is?"

"I don't know what you expect from me."

"I expect my boyfriend to be by my side when my dad is dying."

"And I will be. You can ring me any time and I'll be there."

"Over the phone."

"It's not a five-minute trip down the road, sweetheart. It's the other side of the world."

He glanced at his watch and sighed. "I feel horrible for doing this."

"And yet you're still going."

"Caitlyn…"

"Just go, Marcus. I'll speak to you when I speak to you." He moved his hands to cup my face, but I backed away from him. "Don't. Just go."

Rain started pattering at the windows giving a welcome noise to the strained silence between us. "I'll be back before you know it."

"Yep."

"Caitl—"

"Go, Marcus. You've already wasted enough time remember."

The pain that flickered across his handsome face almost made me feel guilty. Almost. "Can I have a kiss?"

"Are you kidding me? No!"

"Sweetheart, come on."

I exploded like a ball of fire. I'd had enough of him trying to placate me. "I am not your sweetheart." Deep thunder rolled through the skies outside. A gust of wind blew open my apartment door, flinging it back at such a rate, I worried it had been ripped off its hinges. "Get the hell out of my house, Marcus. Now!"

He didn't stay a second longer. Within the blink of an eye he'd vanished, leaving me to deal with the violent whirlwind of emotions tumbling around inside me.

CHAPTER SEVENTEEN

I couldn't believe this. How had my life collapsed around me in such a short space of time? I didn't understand.

"Cat, are you ok?"

I turned and looked at Luke, his whiskey brown eyes full of care and concern, and shrugged my shoulders. "I don't even know what to think right now."

"Do you want a hug?"

I really did, more than anything, but I'd been trying my hardest to deny my feelings for Luke. Being close to him would only make that worse. As much as I'd convinced myself this thing between us was born out of insecurities, I knew deep down it was much more than that. I didn't even know what I had with Marcus anymore, let alone trying to bring Luke into the equation.

"No," I said, shaking my head. "I'm ok."

He cocked his head to one side. "Cat." He held his arms out. "Come on."

More than emotionally battered, I couldn't resist. I needed some comfort and stability. Without a second more of hesitation, I flung myself at him. As soon as he curled his arms around me, I closed my eyes and let out a sigh. Hearing the steady beat of his heart soothed my soul and the warmth of his body radiated peace into my core. I'd never felt more at home than I did in his arms.

That thought alone terrified me through and through. I knew he had feelings for me but that didn't mean I was going to take advantage of it. He'd made it clear that crossing boundaries wasn't acceptable just as much as I had, even if I had been tempted.

"I'm always here for you, Cat. You know that," he whispered, stroking the back of my head.

"I know, thank you."

He hugged me tighter and pressed a kiss to my hair. "You've no need to thank me."

I couldn't hold back the tears then. They leaked out of my eyes, silent, but in streams, soaking his shirt in a matter of minutes.

"Hey," he said, pulling back slightly. He tilted my chin up and said, "Don't cry. You're too pretty to cry, especially over Marcus bloody Davenport."

I giggled. "It's not just him. I just feel very overwhelmed by everything."

"Ok," he said, pushing me back into the solidarity of his chest. "Because he doesn't deserve your tears."

I smiled. The more everything seemed to be unravelling around me, the more I realised I probably had a whole world of lies and revelations to pick my way through. The hardest thing would be knowing who I could trust.

***

Dad looked dreadful. I made it to his room in time just as he woke up. His skin looked sallow and saggy and seemed to have a consistency like tissue paper, as if the slightest thing would tear it beyond repair. Dark circles shadowed his eyes and with his cheekbones protruding he looked ghoulish.

Without a doubt seeing him like this was the worst thing I had ever seen. I couldn't believe this was my dad. In that instant, I knew the veil of death was hanging over him, just waiting for the moment to drop the final curtain. The man I loved all my life was wasting away in front of me and there was nothing I could do to stop it.

Or was there?

Seeing him looking so terrible immediately squashed my appetite but I forced the scrambled eggs and toast down me so he didn't worry there was anything wrong.

"Do you mind if I have a nap before we take a look at the books again?" he asked, even his voice weak and fragile.

"Of course not. I'll go help with the rooms and check back in about an hour."

He patted my hand and closed his eyes, dozing off back to sleep. I bit my lip to stem the flow of tears welling up. If eating exhausted him, how long really did he have left?

As quietly as I could, I crept out of his room and ran upstairs to find Joanna. I found her at the end of the first floor. I guessed she'd used some 'additional' help to get this far in an hour.

"Hey," she said, grinning as she saw me running towards her.

I bundled her into the nearest room and closed the door. "You have to help me."

She frowned. "With what?"

"With my dad. There must be something you can do to stop him dying!"

"We work magic, Cat, not miracles."

"Same thing."

She shook her head. "No, it really isn't. The kindest thing to do would be to alleviate his suffering."

I took a step back. "What?"

"Do you like seeing him in so much pain?"

"Of course not."

"Then wish for it to happen sooner rather than later because he is in agony, Cat."

"I just want my dad," I said, my voice cracking. "There must be something you can do."

Joanna stepped forwards and gave me a hug. "We can't save someone from death when they're this far gone, Cat, I'm sorry. It's his time."

I pulled away and looked her in the eye. "Are you just saying that so his magic gets recycled back?"

Her eyes widened and filled with surprise. "My goodness, no. If we wanted his magic that bad, he'd be dead already." She clamped a hand over her mouth. "I'm sorry. That came out harsher than I expected."

I shook my head. "It's ok. I'm sorry. My head is all over the place today."

"You've had a lot happen in a short space of time." She put her hand on mine and said, "I know Keres gave you a memory unlock potion. Go and give it to him and enjoy the time you have left talking about everything."

I had the vial in my pocket. "Ok, thank you."

"I'm here whenever you need to talk. Go and spend the day doing something fun and clear your mind. I've got the rooms."

"Are you sure?"

"Of course. Now go."

I nodded and wandered back downstairs. I could hear Dad's snores from outside his room. Sophie looked like she had a hand on things in the kitchen which left me at a bit of a loose end. I wandered back through the kitchen and outside, heading to my apartment, when Luke opened my apartment door.

"Ah, there you are," he said, a coy smile on his face. "Come on."

I frowned. "Come on, what?"

"You're coming with me for the day."

"Where?"

"Riding."

I squealed in delight. "You don't have to tell me twice."

He pulled his lips tight and said, "We'll have to take your car though…"

"Ok…not that I mind, but why?"

He scratched the back of his head and said, "Well, I kind of didn't drive over here last night."

"How did you…oh. Really?"

He nodded. "I was rather angry. We're faster than those leeches." He smirked. "I don't think he was expecting me to turn up so quickly."

"Oh, for goodness sake, quit it already with the pissing contest, will you?" I rolled my eyes and turned towards my apartment. "Let me get my keys."

He chuckled. "Stay here. Let me get your keys."

"They're on the—"

"I got it," he said, smiling.

Seconds later he emerged with my keys. He walked around to the passenger side and opened the door. I stood staring at him.

"I'm holding the door open for you," he said.

"It's my car, I'm driving," I said, opening the drivers door.

"Oh no you're not. I don't get driven around by women. It's my job to drive them around."

"Well, today you're redundant."

He snorted. "I don't think so."

"You don't have insurance," I said, giving him a triumphant smile.

"I have a trade policy. I'm covered to drive anything."

I scowled. "My car, I'm driving."

"Fine," he said, throwing me the keys. "But if you don't let me drive, then I'm not letting you ride."

My jaw dropped. "That is so not fair."

He winked. "I can play just as dirty."

I cursed him under my breath. Then, with all the strength I could muster, chucked the keys back at him. He caught them in one hand, cool as a cucumber, and with a stupid Chesire cat grin on his face.

"Just enjoy my chivalry," he said, still holding the door open for me. "There's not much of it left in this world."

I glared at him but said nothing as I climbed into the passenger seat of my own car. He shut the door and chuckled at my seething expression. Karma was yet to come though. He sat in the drivers seat and then looked around the car, his eyes bulging as he took in all the rubbish, loose stones, and bits of fluff.

"Bet you want me to drive now, hmmm?"

"Does a homeless person live in here?" he asked, raising his eyebrows at me.

"Carry on and find out."

He laughed. "Seriously, Cat, this is gross. What is wrong with you?"

"I'm a busy girl. A lot of my food is grab and go."

"And you clearly think you're driving a bin."

"I do remember you offered to clean it actually…"

He wagged his finger from side to side at me. "Oh, no, no, no. We had a pinky promise that if I broke it, this was the punishment. You have no worries about me breaking that promise, that's for sure."

"Chicken."

"No, I just appreciate my health."

"Which considering you're supernatural, you have better health than us humans."

He grinned. "You're not human."

"Goddammit."

He laughed and struck up the engine. He instantly lowered both windows and reversed the car out of its space.

"What are you doing?" I said, pushing the button for my window to go back up.

"Airing it out of any mould spores."

I laughed. "Oh, come on. It's not that bad."

He pushed a button on the drivers side door which locked the windows in place. The freezing October air bit at my cheeks as he drove down the road. I said nothing, intent that he was not going to get the last laugh at this.

"I have another idea," he said, the tone of

amusement in his voice making me want to instantly groan.

"Do I dare even ask?"

I looked at him to see him grinning like an idiot. "Remember that whole thing with the car…"

"What thing with the car?"

"About going to buy a new one in trashy clothes."

I groaned. "No, Luke, no."

"Come on, it'll be fun."

"I don't want to go miles away with Dad being so poorly."

"We won't go miles away. York at the furthest, I promise."

"But that's like an hour and a half away, Luke. What if something happens?"

"Then we come back."

"But it'll take ages."

"Well, where I was planning on going riding is three hours."

I gawped. "Three hours there?"

He nodded.

"Are you lying to me just to get me to agree to this ridiculous car idea?"

He slapped a hand over his heart. "Would I do such a thing?"

"Yes."

"I'm hurt, Cat, genuinely hurt."

"Sure," I said, fighting the urge to smile. "Fine. Let's do it. Shut you up about it at least."

"Are you serious?"

I narrowed my eyes at him. "Don't make me say it again."

He pounded his hands on the steering wheel, clearly excited to say the least. "You've no idea how much you just made my day."

"I'm thinking clearly I have no idea how much I just ruined my day."

CHAPTER EIGHTEEN

Luke turned into a giant kid. I'd never seen a grown man so excited to do something so…weird. When we pulled up at his farmhouse, something familiar and homely enveloped me. I wanted to stay here as long as possible, it was just so pretty and peaceful.

"I think you look grubby enough," he said, giving me the once over.

"Excuse me?"

"Well your top has a hole in it, you've got paint stains on your jeans, and a spot of ketchup at the corner of your mouth."

My face flushed red. I flipped the sun visor down and looked at my reflection. No ketchup. I glared at Luke. "Really?"

"Gotcha."

With that, he leaped out of the car, throwing the keys into my lap. He ran towards the old wooden barn at the side of the house. How the rickety old thing was still standing baffled me.

"Are you coming?" he shouted.

I grinned. Karma, bitch. I pointed at the door and shrugged my shoulders.

His face fell and he jogged back to the car. "I'm sorry. I got a little over excited."

He opened the door for me and I got out. "Looks like chivalry really is dying."

"I know, I'm sorry." He looked down at my trainers and then at the muddy path leading to the barn. Before I knew it, he scooped me up in his arms.

I shrieked in surprise and laughed. "What are you doing?"

He started marching towards the barn. "Hopefully this will make up for my lapse with the door."

"Don't be ridiculous," I said, looking at his handsome face. I found myself resisting the urge to kiss his cheek. I wanted to put my arms around his neck and cuddle into him, but I couldn't. It wouldn't be appropriate. "Besides, some mud on my trainers would only add to the look, right?"

A wicked glint passed through his eyes. "Good point." He promptly put me down, right in the thick of the mud. The ground actually squelched. "Excellent thinking, Cat."

"Oh my God!" I yelled. "Did you actually just do this?"

He carried on walking and yelled back, "Yep, I think I did."

I let out a scream of frustration. These trainers were only four months old, I'd bought them just before coming back to Whitby. Bright white with streaks of purple and pink, I adored them. Now they were just brown. Even the laces.

Luke opened the barn doors to reveal an old red car. The bottom of the rear bumper had more dents in it than a punchbag and the exhaust was rotten. When he got in it, the car creaked and leaned heavily to one side. I couldn't help but giggle.

When he reversed it out, I had to put my hands over my mouth to stop the giggling. The entire side of it was a mangled mix of rust and red paint. Luke looked absolutely ridiculous in it, like a bear who had been crammed into a sardine tin.

"Get in," he shouted through the window.

I opened the door carefully, in case it fell off its hinges, and sat down.

"Hey, you're getting the carpet muddy," he said, chuckling.

I bent down and scraped some of the still wet mud off the side of one of my trainers. "I wonder why?" I said, smearing his cheek with the mud. At least I wouldn't want to kiss it now.

"You didn't just do that?" he said, looking at himself in the rear-view mirror.

"Yep, I think I did."

He wiped most of the mud off his face leaving a brown smear behind. To my horror, he spread it all over my forehead. I screeched like a mouse and batted his hand away.

"You didn't!"

He laughed. "Yep, I think I did."

I rubbed at my forehead, hunching down and looking at myself in the wing mirror. I looked like I'd attempted to put makeup on and forgotten about it.

"Luke, I am not going anywhere looking like this."

"Then how come we're moving?" he said, wiggling his eyebrows up and down.

"Luke! Seriously!"

He laughed. "Calm down. You've got plenty left on your trainers to make the rest of your face match."

I spent the next half an hour licking the fingers on my left hand and rubbing at the mud on my forehead. It didn't do much. You could still tell I had mud on me. I gave up and settled back in the threadbare seat.

"You look adorable," Luke said, trying not to laugh. "I'm sure I'll get a good deal just for how cute you look."

I stuck my tongue out at him and crossed my arms over my chest. "Seriously, mate, you're gonna pay for that."

He laughed. "Mate?"

"Yep, that's what you've been downgraded to."

"As oppose to?"

I opened my mouth to answer but quickly realised I had no answer. "Oh stop it, you know what I meant."

He grinned. "Let's talk about this dream you had that upset Marcus so much."

"I'd really rather not."

"It looks like we're going to be spending a lot of time together so you may as well tell me."

I frowned. "What makes you say that?"

He passed me his phone. On the screen was a message from Marcus. **Look after her whilst I'm gone. Please.**

I snorted and passed it back. "Nice."

"He does care for you, Cat."

"Oh, spare me the sob story. He's in the doghouse for a long time yet."

"Tell me about this dream then."

I sighed and gave in. I detailed him on the dream and everything that happened up until the point where he arrived.

"So how come you guys aren't naked after you've…you know…changed?" I asked.

"Our clothes become part of our fur. When the fur disappears, the clothes are left on."

"Oh, that's quite…cool."

"I do sympathise with him to an extent," Luke said, sighing. "Of course, I'm not going to tell him that."

I giggled. "Why do you sympathise?"

"I've not seen my parents for years so I get where he's coming from with his mum."

I frowned. "You said they're travelling?"

He shook his head. "No, they're not. They're in hiding."

"Why?"

"She's a witch and he's a werewolf."

I took a moment to think about that. How awful must it be to have to hide your love from the world because some stupid rule demanded no love between different species? That was no way to live, not for anyone. "How have you survived on your own?"

"I've had my brothers and sisters, they protected me and hid me from outsiders. It wasn't until I was fully grown that I could fend for myself. People that do know about me have learned I'm no threat so they just pretend I don't exist. I'm happy with that, it beats death or being on the run."

"Or in hiding," I said, giving him a sympathetic smile.

He nodded. "I blamed myself for years for them having to hide. Took me a long time to figure out that they would be in hiding regardless of whether I existed or not. Forever is a long time to hide and not see your own family."

My heart ached for him. I couldn't even begin to imagine what his parents must be going through. "Do wolves...do you live forever too?"

"Yes, werewolves are immortal. We don't turn on a full moon, we turn at will. Silver doesn't kill us, and our bites don't kill vampires."

My curiosity had been piqued. "So what does kill you?"

He laughed. "Are you asking me to tell you how to dispose of me?"

I giggled. "Yes, I think I am."

He grinned. "It's ok," he said, giving me a cheeky wink. "I know you couldn't live without me."

I burst out laughing. "Of course not."

"A wooden stake right through the heart. Problem is getting to it. Our ribcage is ten times stronger than any vampires and our hearts are encased in bone."

I raised my eyebrows. I hadn't expected something so tough. "That's…hardcore."

"Have to be to survive in our world."

I desperately wanted to reach over and take his hand. I felt like he needed comfort right now after touching on the subject of his parents. "How old are you?"

"I stopped ageing at thirty. That was one hundred and twenty years ago."

My jaw dropped. "You're one hundred and fifty?"
He nodded.
"I gotta say, you age pretty good."
He laughed. "Thanks."

"I'm guessing the different mum is why you're built so much…bigger than the rest of your brothers and sisters?"

He nodded. "Yes, but only because she's a witch. With her being a witch mum, I got an extra boost of magic as I was developing in the womb. My size is related to how much of a power boost I got. If Dad had been the witch and Mum the wolf, I'd be just like the rest of my family."

"That's…that must have been hard to grow up with? I sensed a lot of tension between you and Mason."

He smirked. "He's a prick. Always has been, always will be."

"I gathered that," I said, laughing. "Anyway, less talk of the unpleasant things in life. What car are you looking at?"

"I don't know, I'm keeping my options open. I thought about a Range Rover because I'm a big guy, but I kind of like the idea of a sports car. They have some Audi's, Merc's and BMW's in so we'll see."

"Really going low key then," I said, giggling. "How does a handyman earn so much money?"

He laughed. "I've had plenty of years to work and invest my money in the correct places. Don't judge a book by its cover."

"Are you like a millionaire or something then?"

"Why?" he asked, grinning. "Are you a gold digger? Because if you are, the answer is yes."

I burst out laughing. "No, I'm not but that's a good option to know."

We carried on chit chatting for the rest of the drive. When we turned down a little country lane with brand new red brick buildings lining the road, my anxiety shot through the roof. What the hell was I doing? Why had I agreed to do this?

Luke parked right outside the front door, right next to a brand-new Porsche. I nearly choked. "You can't park here," I whispered.

"There's a parking space, Cat, so yes, I think I can."

"Oh my God, I want to crawl in a hole and die," I said, shrinking in my seat.

"Lighten up, have some fun. Come on." He pointed at the open roller shutter door. "There's a whole warehouse of them in there. Let's go have a look."

He opened his car door, and I couldn't help but squeak. "Don't, Luke. Let's just go home."

"Oh, get your big girl knickers on. You're supposed to be some badass witch, right? Prove it."

I frowned. "I'm not entirely sure how I'm supposed to do that when we're car shopping."

"Just get out the car, Cat." He took the keys from the ignition and pushed himself out of the small opening. "Chicken."

I sucked in a deep breath and got out of the car. I glared at him over the roof and said, "You're gonna get downgraded to matey in a minute."

He grinned. "Fine by me, Captain."

"What?"

"Matey is a pirate term."

I grinned. "You know you forgot to open the Captain's door again? You're seriously lacking, matey."

"Get inside, wench."

We headed inside the immaculate showroom, chuckling away like a pair of teenagers. When I took in the sight in front of me, I had to stop and take a moment. I'd never seen such a collection of prestige cars.

Row after row of shiny sports cars. Ferrari, Porsche, Lamborghini, even some names I didn't recognise. I couldn't imagine the money's worth sat in this one place.

"See anything you like?" Luke asked, casually strolling along the first row of cars.

"Yes, but this isn't my car. It's yours."

"I think having an outside opinion would be beneficial."

"My outside opinion would be as long as I don't have to travel in that rot box ever again, buy whatever you fancy."

He laughed. "She's a classic. You leave old Jessie alone."

"Jessie? You named that thing?"

"Yes, it's the law. A man has to name his toys."

I pointed at a bright blue Porsche. "That's a toy. Not that thing out there," I said, jerking my head towards the door.

"How very dare you. Poor Jessie." He skimmed his fingers over the gleaming paintwork on a white car I didn't recognise. "This is…well, Jessie wouldn't come close to this, I have to say."

"What even is it?" I asked, looking at the weird red mark it had for a logo.

"This is a McLaren. The new GT if I'm not mistaken. Brand new out this year."

"It looks expensive."

"That's because they are expensive. You can kiss goodbye to the best part of two hundred grand for one of these."

My jaw dropped. "I could buy a house with that!"

"Hi there."

I turned to see an older gentleman in a grey suit striding towards us. His grey hair had been slicked back with gel and he walked with an air of arrogance I instantly took a dislike to. His beady green eyes were scanning us up and down already.

"Hi," said Luke, holding out his hand.

The man looked at it and pressed his hands together. "I'm sorry. Bit of a germ freak. My name is Owen. Can I help you?"

I glanced at Luke with a wicked glint in my eye. He gave me the smallest of nods. "Hi, Owen. I'm Caitlyn." I put my finger on the McLaren and walked down the side, sliding my finger across the smooth paintwork. "We really like this car."

He scratched his head and coughed. "Please don't touch the paintwork, Miss. That's a very expensive car."

I resisted the urge to smirk. This guy was so pretentious and clearly looking down his nose at us. "Oh, I know. I have a choice of what car to buy. A gift from my darling boyfriend."

"Well," he said, coughing and clapping his hands together. "Why don't I show you our selection of second-hand cars out the back? I'm sure they'll be at a more comfortable price point for you."

"I'm sorry?"

Worry filled his little piggy eyes. "Just…you know," he said, motioning his hand over us both. "I'm sure these cars are perhaps a little out of your league."

I looked at Luke and smirked. "Did you hear that, darling? This car is out of our league."

Luke nodded and looked at the man. "Maybe you'll just indulge my girlfriend's desire to appreciate nice cars?"

"Yes, of course," Owen said. "But please no touching."

"Hands in pockets," I said, grinning at him and making a point of shoving them into my jeans.

"Enjoy," he said, before retreating back to the office.

"Wow," I whispered to Luke. "Can you believe that? You were right though. That was fun watching him twitch as I touched it."

He laughed. "Told you. The best bit hasn't even started yet."

"What are you talking about?"

"Watch and learn, Cat. Watch and learn."

CHAPTER NINETEEN

We wandered along the rows of cars for ages. Luke paid particular interest in a blue BMW and a black Audi. As he stood back admiring the two, a green Range Rover pulled up outside the shutter doors. A young man jumped out of the drivers seat, his black hair carefully styled into a quiff. He also wore a grey suit but his smile and general energy came across as nothing but warm and friendly.

"Hi there, folks. I'm Ryan. Can I help you?"

Luke offered his hand. "I'm Luke. This is Caitlyn."

Ryan didn't hesitate to shake Luke's hand. "Nice to meet you both. Have you seen anything you like?"

"I'm quite taken with these two to be honest," Luke said. "I was debating a Range Rover, I'm not a small guy, but I like the sleek look these two have."

Ryan walked over to the Audi. "This is an

excellent choice if I may say so myself. It has an air of sophistication to it which I can tell is something you appreciate." He then went to the BMW. "This is sporty and a world of fun. You strike me as the type of gentleman who likes to get the most from his cars."

"You would be correct."

"Why don't you take them both for a test drive? Swap over halfway so you both get a feel for them?"

I glanced at Luke, surprised that Ryan was including me in this but the excitement bubbling inside me was hard to ignore.

"That would be fantastic, thank you," Luke said.

"I'll just go get the keys."

As he marched back to the office, I resisted the urge to scream. "I can't believe I'm going to drive them!"

Luke narrowed his eyes. "You better not damage them or there will be trouble."

"Hey, matey, I'm the Captain. I ace being in charge of powerful expensive cars."

"Cat, I'm serious."

"Oh, lighten up, Frodo."

He raised an eyebrow and laughed. "What did you just call me?"

"Frodo."

"As in the hobbit?"

"Yep."

He folded his arms over his chest. "Do I look like a hobbit to you?"

"You don't look like one but you're definitely acting like one. Are you going to turn all Gollum on me?"

He laughed. "I'm not going to even dignify that with an answer."

"That'll be a yes then."

"Here's the keys for you," Ryan said, striding towards us. "Who wants to take what first?"

"Audi," I said, my eyes lighting up.

Luke pulled a face at me and snatched the keys for the BMW. "Is there a set route or anything?"

Ryan gave him directions for a ten-mile round trip as I opened the door on the Audi. I looked up to see Owen scowling at us through the window of the office. I glanced down at my crusty muddy trainers and struggled not to laugh. Without a doubt, he'd definitely be twitching now.

I sat down in the black leather seat and swallowed the moan of pleasure that rose in my throat. It had 'RS' stitched into the seat and amazing honeycomb padding. Solid but soft, comfortable but hugged my body, I could fall asleep in this seat and wake feeling perfectly refreshed. The steering wheel had all sorts of buttons and controls on it and the touch screen in the centre of the dash looked awfully high-tech.

"Are you ok with starting it?" Ryan asked, coming over to me. "Double tap the engine start button, put your foot on the brake, and then press the button again."

I looked down at the dash and spotted the engine start button. When I double tapped it, the dash in front of the steering wheel lit up in a beautiful digital display. I bit my lip in an effort to stem the elation coursing through my veins.

Once I started it, the roar of the engine made my heart backflip. It sounded powerful, to a scary degree. Luke pulled in front of me, already good to go in the BMW, and put his thumb up. I nodded, moved the gearstick into drive, and eased the car out of its space.

When we were down the little lane, well away from the garage, I let out a scream of joy. I couldn't believe I was actually driving a car like this. I had well and truly fallen in love. We turned left at the top of the lane, driving into what looked like more country roads. As Luke turned the BMW left, he accelerated at such a speed, he left me covered in dust. Part of me wanted to follow his lead but the sensible side of me kept the car plodding along. I couldn't risk losing control of something like this and crashing it.

Luke tore off into the distance, seemingly enjoying the curves in the road as he threw it around the twisty bends. I chugged along at the speed limit, desperate to try its power but more mindful of my life and Luke's reaction if I damaged it.

A few minutes later, Luke pulled over into a field entrance. I pulled up next to him, realising he wanted to swap over.

"What do you think?" he said, jumping out of the BMW.

"I have no words," I replied, grinning like an idiot. "It's absolutely beautiful."

"See what you think to that one then." He jumped into the driving seat of the Audi. "Don't scratch it."

"Hey, I didn't scratch that one."

"I just wanted to make it clear."

I rolled my eyes. "Yes, Meredith."

His jaw dropped. "I can't believe you just called me that."

I slid into the drivers seat of the BMW and looked at him. "Believe it, pal, 'coz it just happened."

"Pal?"

I grinned and shut the door.

Frowning at me, he pulled off in the Audi at a

ridiculous speed, kicking up dirt and tiny stones. I found myself shrieking and holding the steering wheel in a pathetic attempt to protect the car, then realised what a twerp I was being.

I carefully drove off the field entrance and eased the car up to sixty. This felt so different to the Audi. Everything felt aggressive and urgent. It had two little red buttons on the steering wheel marked M1 and M2. They almost gave me heart palpitations at the thought of touching them. The digital dash also projected onto the windscreen, making it quite distracting from the road. I didn't feel as relaxed and chilled in this; I felt like I was on the edge of racing at any point.

Luke seemed to be enjoying the Audi though, giving it the same treatment he had done this. They were both absolutely stunning cars though. My pick would be the Audi; I felt safe and comfortable in it. Whilst the BMW was just as gorgeous, it seemed to be aimed more for the people who enjoyed speed and living life a little closer to the edge.

As we turned back down the little lane to the garage, Ryan stepped outside, a big smile on his face. Luke pulled up behind the Range Rover and hopped out of the Audi, heading straight to Ryan. I brought the BMW to a stop and switched it off, breathing a sigh of relief. It actually scared me but this wasn't my choice of my car. I had a feeling which one Luke had his heart set on.

I got out of the BMW and headed towards Luke.

"What do you think?" Ryan asked.

I was surprised he wanted my opinion but also impressed he cared. "I prefer the Audi. The BMW is too 'racy' for me."

He chuckled. "A lot of women say that."

"I think the BMW is more of a driver's car. It's raw and ready to go," Luke said, looking at them both. "The Audi is refined and sophisticated but still delivers power when you need it. Although it is markedly less than the BMW."

Ryan nodded. "I couldn't have said it better myself. The Audi RS5 was built to compete with the BMW M5 but BMW have hit the nail on the head every time with the M series. They never fail to deliver a driver's car. If that's what you're looking for, there is no comparison."

Luke sighed. "Ideally I'd take bits from both of them and build my own perfect car. I need the engine from the BMW in the Audi."

"If its raw power you're after but with an Audi badge, have you considered an R8?"

Luke chuckled. "I don't think that's my kind of car. I'm not in a mid-life crisis just yet."

Ryan laughed. "We have one if you want to take it for a test drive."

"I couldn't picture myself with one of those but thank you for the offer."

"Is there anything else that caught your eye?"

Luke pressed his lips together. "If I was buying for the sake of buying, then the McLaren, but that's not practical. These two have the capability to be everyday cars as well as something a bit special."

"I agree. Do you want to talk it over with your girlfriend, or go away and think about it?"

When Ryan said 'girlfriend' my heart somersaulted. Part of me wanted to jump in and say 'hey, we're just friends' but another part of me wanted to let it go. I decided on keeping quiet. Now was not the time to address our complicated friendship.

"No," Luke said. "I think I've decided."

Ryan nodded. "A man who knows what he wants."

"Yes, indeed. I'll take both."

I gasped and stumbled backwards.

Ryan faltered for the slightest of moments before holding his hand out. "An excellent choice. I'll go and sort the paperwork."

As Ryan hurried back inside the building, I walked over to Luke, my heart racing, and said, "What the hell?"

He grinned. "I love them both. I couldn't decide. This way I'm not going to wonder if I chose right because I'll have the two of them. And change to spare," he said, winking.

"How are we getting three cars back home?" I asked.

"I doubt we'll be taking these today. They'll need to prep them and stuff."

"Please don't tell me I've got to get back in that rot box after being in these?"

Luke grinned. "You leave Jessie alone. She's a good old girl."

"You know what you've done, don't you?"

"What?"

"You've taken me to the Ritz for a starter and to McDonalds for the main course."

He tipped his head back and laughed. When he looked at me, he burst into more laughter. "What an analogy."

"It's true. I feel cheated. I've had fifteen, maybe twenty minutes in complete luxury, and now I have to slum it for an hour and a half back home."

"I am quite hungry actually. Do you fancy a

McDonalds?"

I smirked and narrowed my eyes at him. "I'm sure I remember Joanna telling me that when her first boyfriend upset her, she put a spell on his…you know…and turned it green. I wonder if she'd teach me how to do that?"

"You wouldn't dare."

I grinned. "Is that a challenge?"

"No!" he shouted. "It certainly is not."

"Do you still fancy a McDonalds?"

He pouted. "No. And I was looking forward to a Big Mac."

I smiled. "You can have one if we're not in that death trap."

He frowned. "Let me get this straight. I can't have a greasy burger in a rotten old car, but I can have one in a car that's cost a hundred grand. What makes you think that makes sense or that I'd even allow food to be eaten in either of those cars?"

I thought for a split second before replying, "Because I'm the Captain, matey. And what I say goes."

He turned away from me, muttering under his breath.

"What was that?" I asked, smiling.

"I said I need to ring the bank."

I giggled to myself. I felt mean but not mean enough to apologise. Luke had been right about one thing though—this had definitely been fun.

CHAPTER TWENTY

An hour later, we were heading towards McDonalds. The best bit was old Jessie had been left behind. Result. As we turned onto the main road, I couldn't help but grin at what had just happened.

When it came to paying, Luke called his bank and instructed them on the amount, which nearly made me choke, and to send it as a faster payment so we could take the cars with us there and then.

Ryan had not been sheepish at all when he told Luke the amount—one hundred and seventy-nine thousand, two hundred and five pounds. Luke casually nodded and called the bank. I felt like fainting.

However, when Luke instructed the bank to send over two hundred thousand pounds flat, I actually sat down on the nearest chair I could find. Ryan's jaw dropped and Owen looked like he'd just been tasered with the shock on his face.

After Luke ended the call, he looked Owen straight in the eye and said, "The extra is a tip for this young man. If I find out he's not got every single penny, I'll be coming to pay you a visit."

Owen just nodded, he looked too shell shocked to say anything.

Ryan had tears in his eyes. "I can't thank you enough. My wife and I are saving up for a deposit on a house."

Luke smiled and patted him on the shoulder. "Well you use that as you see fit. You deserve it. Thank you for your attention today."

As Owen sat in the office, checking the bank every five minutes, Ryan took all the sale stickers off the cars, put the correct documents in them, did a final wipe over with a soft cloth and some sort of spray, and shook both our hands. The delight in his eyes was hard to miss. Luke had literally just made his day, or probably his year.

Going round the McDonalds drive-through in a prestige car felt awfully strange. After Luke got his food, he drove into a car parking space. I pulled up next to him, desperate to eat my quarter pounder with cheese.

I dropped the passenger side window and said, "What's wrong?"

He got out of the BMW, with his food, and jumped into the passenger seat of the Audi. "I don't mind one car stinking of fast food but not both."

I laughed. "Funny that it's the Audi you chose for that."

"I can't have the smell of fast food distracting me from such an awesome car. It goes without saying it was going to be the Audi."

"I still can't believe you bought both of these. Are you insane?"

"No," he said, biting into his Big Mac. "Just enjoying the spare money I have."

I started munching on some chips. Spare money to me was having ten quid leftover, not two hundred grand. I couldn't help but wonder if there was a 'get rich quick' spell. I'd have to ask Joanna.

We ate in comfortable silence and headed for home, but not after Luke told me to drive his new car carefully.

"No speeding, no overtaking, don't go anywhere near a curb either."

I rolled my eyes. "I got it."

As we pulled back onto the main road, the first thing he did was overtake four cars and a tractor. Remembering his rule of 'no overtaking', I sat behind the tractor, even after the other cars had gone around it. About ten minutes later, my phone rang.

I pressed 'Answer' on the touch screen dash and in the sweetest voice I could muster, I said, "Hello."

"What the hell are you doing?" Luke said.

"You told me no overtaking."

Silence. Then I heard a long breath being let out. "Cat, get your arse around that tractor, now."

"Are you giving me permission to overtake?"

He hung up.

Giggling hysterically to myself, I dared to hit the accelerator hard and hung on to the steering wheel with both hands. The car lurched forwards from the sudden power burst, pinning me back in my seat. As it kept on accelerating, I found myself rather addicted to the power this thing had. When I hit ninety-five and caught up with Luke, I debated for a split second overtaking him, then thought better of it.

Then thought better of that.

I shrieked with part joy, part fear, as I shot past him, daring to wave with my left hand. His face was a picture. He looked like he'd just been introduced to running water. I waited for the phone call, but it didn't happen. Instead, I heard an almighty roar as he came blasting past me and dived back in front. I could see his eyes in the rear-view mirror, glaring. I had no doubt that if looks could kill, I'd be dismembered by now.

Like a meek little lamb, I followed him perfectly, not putting a foot out of place all the way back to his. When I got out of the car, my heart started pounding. He was going to go mental at me for that, I just knew it.

He jumped out of the BMW and marched over to me, holding his hands out for the key. "You are so antagonistic, you know that, right?"

"I try my best," I said, giving him a little curtsy.

He narrowed his eyes at me. "Don't you ever overtake me in one of my cars again."

"Is this just some macho thing about a man needing to be better than a woman? You were in the faster car. I don't see wh—"

He grabbed my waist and pulled me into him. Before I could even think, his lips were on mine. I was stunned. No tongues involved or even a warm embrace, just his mouth on mine, kissing me. I didn't know what to say or do. When he pulled away and stepped back, I could see shock filtering through his eyes.

Quickly recovering, he chuckled and said, "Finally, I shut you up."

I couldn't even laugh. I was numb. However, I

couldn't help but wonder if that had been a tactic to shut me up or if it meant something more. *No, Cat. Don't go down that road. It didn't mean anything. Home. I need to go home.*

"I…um…." I looked up at him, shocked and confused "…home. Yes, I need to go home."

Fishing my car keys out of my pocket, I walked over to my car, somewhat in a daze, and sat down in it. On nothing but autopilot, I somehow managed to start it, and drive myself home. I didn't know what to think or feel.

I wandered into the house, the delicious aroma of chicken curry filling my nose—one of Dad's favourites.

"Hey, Sophie," I said, my head still all over the place.

"Hey, Cat. You hungry?"

"Always got room for your curry."

She smiled. "Your dad's awake. I'll bring some through when it's ready."

I felt guilty then that I'd been out for the day with Luke. Dad must have been wondering where I was.

"Pumpkin," he said, as I stepped through the door. "Had a good day?"

He looked so much brighter. His skin had a pink flush to it and his eyes even had a twinkle in them. "I've been car shopping with Luke."

"Very nice. No Marcus?"

I'd forgotten all about him leaving until then. It hit me right in the heart like a poison arrow. Was it bad that I'd not thought about him all day? Or had I just expected him to be here when I got back?

"No. He's gone away for a few days on business."

"Ah, no rest for the wicked."

I smiled. "How long have you been awake?"

"Not long. Fifteen minutes maybe. The smell of Sophie's curry woke me up. No way I'm missing that."

We chit chatted until Sophie brought her curry in to us. I tried to give Dad my full attention, but Marcus dominated the forefront of my thoughts. He couldn't have actually gone. He wouldn't. Not now, not when I needed him the most. Would he?

"Could you fetch me the salt, please?" Dad said.

The vial. This was my chance to bring back his memories. "Sure. I'll take your bowl for you and put some in."

"Thanks, pumpkin," he said, patting my hand.

My heart racing, I headed into the kitchen. Would I get away with this with Sophie being around?

"Everything ok?" she asked, looking at the bowl.

I nodded. "He just wants some salt."

She tutted. "Him and his salt."

I put the bowl down on the worktop and reached for the salt. Sophie took some plates and cutlery into the dining room giving me my opportunity. I sucked in a deep breath, took the vial from my pocket, and emptied the contents into his curry. That was it done. I sprinkled some salt on top and headed back into his room, the empty vial crammed back in my pocket.

As Dad devoured the delicious food, I sat watching him, full of anticipation. How would it happen? Would it be a sudden surge of memories or flashbacks of moments? When he suggested we watch some more Midsummer Murders, I wondered if the potion would even work at all. Something about this whole scenario reminded me of the film, The Witches, where they put poison in the soup. But that's not what I'd done to Dad. I was trying to create a bridge between him and his previous life before he died.

We watched several episodes of his boxset before he turned to me and said, "I love you, Caitlyn. You're the best thing that ever happened to me and your mum."

Rather taken aback, I stilled for a couple of seconds before kissing his cheek and cuddling him. "I love you too, Daddy. I couldn't have asked for better parents."

He patted my head. "You know don't you, pumpkin?"

My heart froze for a second. it had worked. The potion had worked. I couldn't help but grin. "Yes."

He looked at me and said, "Don't get caught up in all that witchy business. It's not good. You know who you can trust. He's a good man."

"You know he's a—"

"I know he's immortal," Dad said, nodding. "He's honest, hardworking, and he thinks the world of you. I've seen the way he looks at you, right from the first day you met. He's the one for you, Cat. Your soulmate. There's something about the way you two are together that just screams something special. Don't lose it."

I took hold of his hand and squeezed it. "I won't. I can't believe I can finally talk to you about all this." I bit my lip in excitement. "Dad, you need to talk to me about this witch stuff. Spells and potions and all of that."

He chuckled. "I can tell you're excited, pumpkin. You teach yourself, don't let anyone try and teach you. That's the number one rule."

Confused, I frowned. "How am I supposed to learn?"

He pointed a bony finger towards his bookcase.

"I have a safe behind there. It contains five generations of journals from my family. Your mum has even more from her side. That is all you need."

"But my magic is bound."

"Yes, it is," he said, nodding. "You understand we had to do that? If we didn't, you wouldn't be here now."

"I know, I understand. It's ok, Dad. I'm not mad. If anything, I'm just glad we can finally talk about this," I said, water glazing over my eyes.

"You have the power in you to unbind yourself alone. Don't let them fill your head with nonsense."

"What do you mean? I met them. They seem ok. Even Joanna is one."

He smiled. "Oh, yes, she definitely is. She the one who gave you that potion?"

I grimaced. "You know about that?"

He chuckled. "We wouldn't be talking like this right now otherwise." He covered my hand with both of his. "Thank you, Caitlyn."

"For what?"

"The potion, of course. I've been aching for the sweet release of death for days."

My heart froze. Panic swamped me in an instant. A wave of nausea climbed up my throat. "What?"

He patted my hand and smiled. "It's ok, pumpkin. I'm good with this."

"No, Dad. What are you talking about?" My entire body broke out into a cold sweat. My mind raced at a hundred miles an hour with possibilities but deep down, I knew exactly what he was saying.

"The potion. Releasing someone's memories is a dangerous thing to do, especially to someone in my state. It shocks the system." He scrutinised me then, horror filling his eyes. "Joanna didn't tell you that, did she?"

My hands flew to my mouth and I burst into tears. Had I been tricked into killing my own Dad? "It wasn't Joanna, it was Keres."

Dad sat bolt upright and grabbed my arm with a sudden burst of energy that took me by surprise. "Whatever you do, do NOT trust that woman. Do you hear me?" I looked at him completely gobsmacked. He shook my arm, the grip he had on me actually hurting. "Do you understand, Caitlyn?"

"Yes, yes, I understand. Why?"

He collapsed back against his pillows and coughed. I jumped off the bed and handed him a glass of water from his bedside table.

"Are you ok?"

He nodded. "I'm fine. I'm more worried about you. That woman is a demon, Caitlyn. Perfect irony that she's the one to take me down, and through my own daughter too." He shook his head. "Promise me you'll stay away from her."

"Ok, ok. I promise."

"She's nothing but power hungry. All she wants is your power and she'll do anything to get it."

"I'm so sorry. If I'd have known, I would have thrown it away." I covered my face with my hands and resisted the urge to punch myself in the head. "I can't believe what I've done."

"What you've done is given me relief, Cat. You've given me back a lifetime of memories and put me out of my misery."

I flung my arms around him and cried. "There must be something to reverse all this."

He patted my head. "When it's time, it's time."

"How much time do we have?"

"From point of ingestion to death, any point up to twelve hours."

"She made it sound like it'd be days," I said, crying. "I'm so sorry."

He wrapped his arms around me and said, "Don't be. I've told you that."

A knock on the door interrupted what precious time I had left with my dad. I lifted my head and snapped, "What?"

Luke's familiar warm face popped through the open door. "Hey, you left your phone in my car," he said. His eyes filled with concern when he looked at me. "Are you ok?"

I shook my head. "No." I started crying again.

He came in and closed the door behind him. "Hey, Brian. How are you feeling?"

Dad stroked my hair and said, "I'm on top of the world. Cat isn't though."

Luke sat in the chair at the side of Dad's bed and stroked my back. "What's up?"

I opened my mouth to tell him, but I couldn't even speak without bursting into more tears. How could they do this to me? What possible gain did they have from killing my dad? I didn't know who to trust anymore. Marcus had abandoned me, the witches were playing with my head, even Luke and Joanna had lied to me by not telling me their truths.

Dad took the lead and explained to Luke what had happened. The taut silence after he'd finished told me all I needed to know about Luke's reaction.

"It's not your fault, Cat," Luke said, putting his hand on my shoulder.

I didn't bother replying. Why did I trust so easily?

I should have known better. The way Keres had spoken about me being so powerful, I should have realised she'd have her own gains from this. I vowed right then and there to have that fickle head of hers on a stake if it was the last thing I did.

"Do you want to call Marcus?" Luke said.

My whole body tensed up at hearing his name. "No."

"Cat, he said you could call him whenever."

I shook my head. I still refused to believe he'd gone. If I went to his, I knew I'd find him there. He'd be sat outside on his balcony, enjoying the views with some vintage wine in a goldfish bowl for a glass.

"Come here," Dad said, patting the empty bed next to him. "Let's watch some more Midsummer Murders."

"No, Daddy. We need to talk."

"I've said all I need to say. Now come and hug your old Dad whilst we watch some more of this."

I glanced back at Luke. I couldn't do this on my own. "Will you stay?"

His eyes filled with care and he gave me such a warm smile, I actually shivered. "You didn't even need to ask."

I smiled in reply before climbing into the empty spot next to my dad. I settled my head on his shoulder and tried to enjoy the moment rather than worrying about what those damn witches had done. They could be dealt with any time. This time with my dad was precious.

Dad pressed a kiss to the top of my head and then hit play. We watched two full episodes before my eyelids started drooping. The steady rise and fall of my dad's breathing lulled me into a sedative state.

Combined with my eyes being sore from crying and my head on the verge of exploding, I needed some sleep, but I really didn't want to.

I promised myself I would ease the stinging from my eyes with just a brief ten second reprieve. Unfortunately, within about three seconds, sleep claimed me.

When I opened my eyes again, the TV was still playing but it was dark, and deathly quiet. I lifted my head to see Luke dozing in the chair, his chin on his chest. I looked down at Dad. His eyes were closed, and his skin had lost its warmth. I put my hand to my mouth, stemming the cry lodged in my throat, and stared at his chest, waiting to see it rise and fall.

But of course, it didn't.

"Dad," I yelled, shaking him. His head shook from side to side, but it didn't rouse him. "Dad, wake up!" I shook him again but nothing. "Daddy! Daddy, no!"

Luke sprung to life and took over, feeling for a pulse. He looked at me and shook his head. "I'm sorry, Cat."

I burst into tears and put my hands on Dad's emaciated shoulders, shaking him violently. "Wake up, goddammit, Daddy!" I kissed his cheek and put my hands on either side of his face. "Please wake up. Daddy, please!"

Nothing. He was gone.

CHAPTER TWENTY-ONE

Everything that followed was a blur. Luke hugged me until I had no more tears to cry. Then he sat me down in the corner of the room with a blanket and a cup of sugary tea. Like an absolute hero, he took control of everything. He called the doctor, he dealt with the guests, he called Sophie and Joanna and gave them the day off.

The weather outside just added to my bleak mood. Dark clouds hung over the bay, pouring rain like I'd never seen. The pitter patter of it hitting the window almost hypnotised me. I just sat staring at my dad's lifeless body, willing him to suddenly leap back to life and say, "Haha, got ya!" but of course, that didn't happen. The doctor took hours to arrive. It had been around four a.m. when I woke up. He finally appeared at nine. After officially declaring Dad dead, he gave me his condolences and said he'd sort the medical certificate for the cause of death as soon as he got back to the office.

"Don't worry about a thing," Luke said, kneeling down in front of me. "I'll sort it all out, ok?"

I finally tore my gaze from Dad's body and said, "You don't need to do that. Really, it's ok."

He took hold of my hands and looked me square in the eye. "Cat, I want to do it. I don't want you worrying about anything."

The softness in his eyes hit a chord right in my heart. I could see the affection and care he had for me in that moment. It made me want to cry all over again. "Ok, thank you."

"Do you want me to call your mum?"

I hadn't even thought about Mum. I'd been so numb and dazed, I hadn't been capable of thinking anything, let alone logically.

"Please."

He picked up my phone from Dad's desk and scrolled through the contacts. I didn't even care that Mum might freak out at some strange man calling her from her daughter's phone. I just wasn't capable of doing anything except being…blank.

"Hi, Mrs Summers?" A pause. "Hi, my name is Luke Freeman, I'm one of your husband's employees." Another pause. "Yes, Caitlyn is fine. Well, not really. I'm afraid Brian passed away in the early hours. I think she could really use you right about now." Another brief pause. "Ok, I'll let her know."

He put the phone down and sat back in front of me. "Your mum is going to get some things together and head straight up. It'll likely be tonight before she gets here."

I nodded. "Thank you."

"Do you want to go and lay down?"

I shuddered. The thought of being cold and alone right now really didn't appeal to me. "No."

"You look exhausted, Cat."

I shook my head. "I…" my voice cracked "…I don't want to be alone right now."

"Ok, ok." He rubbed his hand up and down my arm. "We'll wait until the funeral home have been and then I'll take you to bed. I won't go anywhere, I promise."

I nodded. I didn't even have the energy to make a joke about him taking me to bed. Insinuations about our complicated friendship were the last thing either of us needed right now.

Sometime around eleven a.m., the funeral home came to collect Dad. When they put him in that black bag, something inside me just snapped as they did the zip up. I jumped from my chair, sending my cup of tea flying, and ran to the metal gurney.

"Don't, don't, please don't take him. He belongs here," I said, looking up at the older gentlemen with a bald head and glasses.

"I know this is hard, sweetheart, but we need to prepare him."

I started crying then as I knew exactly what he meant—pumping him full of chemicals. "I don't…I can't…please."

Luke wrapped his arms around me from behind and then turned me into his chest. I heard the wheels of the gurney rolling across the floor. I dug my fingers in Luke's broad back and screamed for all I was worth. He did nothing but hold me tighter. Outside, the crack of lightning and the rumble of thunder helped drown out the noise of the gurney being taken down the steps.

By the time the skies quietened again, the funeral home people had gone.

"Come on," he said, kissing the top of my head. "Let's get you some sleep."

He walked me through the kitchen and out to my apartment. As soon as we walked inside, I couldn't help but feel cold. Suddenly this place didn't have the charm it once did. I didn't want to be in here.

"I don't want to be in here," I said, burying my head in his chest and shaking my head. "There's some empty rooms on the top floor."

He didn't say a word, just guided me back through the house. When he picked me up to carry me up the stairs, I sighed in relief. I wound my arms around his neck and rested my head on his shoulder.

"Is the suite empty?" he asked.

"I think so."

He took me into the room, which had been Dad's room at one point, and laid me down on the king size bed. The bright blue and white décor immediately felt cosy and familiar. The fluffy pillows and the soft duvet brought half a smile to my face. The window, which faced the bay, was covered in rain, but even with the miserable weather, it was still a refreshing view of the real world.

Luke tugged at my shoes, taking them off my feet and then said, "Are you sleeping clothed?"

I just wanted to close my eyes and forget about all of this. "I can't sleep in my jeans."

He pressed his lips together and then said, "Are you taking them off?"

"Can you? Please?"

He sucked in a deep breath but did as I asked. As he pulled them off my legs, I managed to find the energy to get under the duvet. Luke locked the door then came back to the bed and laid next to me, on top of the quilt.

I looked at him and frowned. "What are you doing?"

"What do you mean?"

"You can't hug me properly through a quilt."

He let out a breath and slid under the duvet. "I swear to God you're trying to kill me."

That did make me smile. Luke wrapped his arms around me and even entwined his legs with mine. Curled up in his warmth, I managed to drift off into a peaceful sleep.

***

By the time I woke up, night had fallen outside. Luke's steady breathing and warm body made me want to stay here forever.

"Hey," he said. "How are you feeling?"

My head still buried in his chest, I asked, "How did you know I was awake?"

"Your breathing changed."

I was a little shocked to say the least. "Oh. You pay attention to things like that?"

He held his breath for a few seconds before whispering, "I pay attention to everything when it concerns you."

I froze. My heart pounded against my ribcage. That had to be one of the sweetest things I'd ever had said to me. I didn't know what to say so I said nothing.

"Your mum called," he said. "Hannah wants to come and see you so they're both going to drive up here tomorrow. Should be here around lunchtime."

Mentally, I let out a sigh of relief. "Ok. Does that mean I get to stay here for a bit longer?"

He squeezed me tight and rubbed his hands up and down my back. "Yes, just a little bit. I need to go and feed the horses."

"They've got acres of grass."

"That is true, but they have a routine, and I don't want to upset them by breaking it."

I moved my head back so I could see his handsome face and said, "Is there something else going on you're not telling me about?"

He met my eyes and sighed. "Do you really want to hear this?"

"Just tell me, please."

He sighed and after a brief pause, said, "I'm going crazy over here, Cat, and I need a break."

I put my hand over my mouth to stifle a giggle. "Are you being serious?"

He leaned back and said, "Are you being serious? You're half naked, Caitlyn. There's only so much willpower a man has."

I did laugh then. "Ok, fair enough. I can't see that Marcus would be too happy if he walked in and saw this."

"Good point," he said, pulling me back into him. "Maybe I should take my shirt off."

"Luke," I said, laughing. "Come on, how would you feel if the shoe was on the other foot?"

He pulled away, untangling our legs and sighed. "I'd be heartbroken. If you were mine, I'd be absolutely heartbroken if you preferred being comforted by someone else."

I shrugged my shoulders. "But Marcus isn't here. I don't have a choice."

He smirked. "Are you saying you're slumming it with me because he's not here?"

"Stop twisting my words, matey."

"There she is," he said, brushing my hair back from my face. "If you were mine and I ever put you in a situation to be comforted by someone else, I'd be heartbroken. Is that better?"

My heart skipped a beat. I knew he meant every word. As much as I was loving this moment, I now fully understood why he insisted on boundaries.

"Do you think we've crossed a line?" I asked.

"I don't know anymore, Cat. I'm fed up with fighting my feelings. It physically pains me."

I looked away and pushed myself further away from him. "Luke, I can't have this conversation right now."

"I know," he said, sighing. "I'm sorry. I think I should go. If you need me, call me."

I nodded. "Thank you for sorting everything today. I do appreciate it."

He slipped his boots back on and stood up. "I'll message you later."

"Ok."

As the door clicked shut behind him, I suddenly felt very alone and very trapped. I fought the part of me that wanted to run down the stairs after him and beg him to stay. Clearly our friendship had somehow developed into more without anything really happening. Even so, I still had Marcus and now all this with Dad to deal with. I didn't need any more complications for a good while yet.

I looked at my phone to see it was seven p.m. Despite my long sleep, I didn't feel refreshed at all. My eyes felt like golf balls and my stomach cramped with hunger pains. I decided in a moment of loneliness to call Marcus. He needed to know Dad had gone and maybe hearing his voice would give me some comfort, even if I couldn't see him.

The line rang, but there was no answer. I tried again. No answer. I tried calling him another three times, each time no different than the last. Anxiety took hold of me then. Why wasn't he answering? Maybe he was actually at home and had left his phone somewhere. After all, he wouldn't have actually gone anywhere. Not at a time like this. The more I thought about him not being there when I needed him, the more I panicked.

I pulled my jeans on and galloped down the stairs. Desperation my only driving force, I grabbed my car keys and sped over to his house. He would be there; I knew he would. He had to be.

"Please be there, please be there," I muttered to myself over and over.

I screeched to a halt on the driveway, sending gravel showering over the landscaped grass. Running to the front door, I almost screamed with joy when it opened. He was here, just like I knew he would be. I ran upstairs, shouting his name, and straight to his bedroom. When I opened the door, I nearly fell backwards.

Everything had a dust sheet on it. Even the bed.

"No, no, no, no," I cried, running from room to room only to find the exact same thing behind every closed door.

He'd done it. He'd gone. I couldn't believe it. His house, once so warm and cosy, filled with so much of his essence, was nothing but an empty shell. There was no indication he'd ever been here, leaving me wondering if I'd imagined the past few months of my life. Had I lost my heart and soul to a vivid imagination, a fictional boyfriend I'd only ever dreamed could be real?

I ran, throwing all caution to the wind, to the one place he knew I feared, he knew I was terrified of without him by my side—the Abbey. If he sensed that's where I was going, if he was anywhere nearby, he'd come for me, to save me, to stop me facing those petrifying memories from years ago.

When I reached the curtain wall of the grounds, my lungs burning for oxygen, I paused and glanced at my nemesis in front of me. To see him again, to have him near me, to be the damsel in distress, I would face this damn heap of stones and force him to come back to me.

Leaping over the boundary wall, I stalked towards the historic ruin in front of me, ignoring all the screaming fears in my mind telling me to go back. I scanned over the empty field around me, hoping to see him striding towards me under the lunar light, coming to save me, his face creased into that familiar worry line.

But he didn't come.

I wandered aimlessly around that old building, my irrational fears of the black wolf gradually calming with each lonely step I took but instead replaced with a rising panic of no Marcus that increased with every second. Eventually, after what felt like hours, I collapsed into a heap and sobbed my heart out.

CHAPTER TWENTY-TWO

Sunlight burned through my eyelids. I opened my eyes to find myself in bed, surrounded by a soft duvet and a heap of pillows. It wasn't my bed; I'd somehow ended up back in the suite, but I didn't care. It was comfy. I realised I was fully clothed as I yawned. Stretching my arms and legs, I revisited yesterday's memories, only to have them come crashing down on me with the force of a freight train.

An aching empty hole sat in the middle of my chest, searing pain tugging at my heart and soul. He was gone. Marcus had left me. Right when I needed him the most. Anger bit at me. If that was the only emotion I had to help me through this, then so be it. I could only cope with losing one important person at once.

I remembered then, what I'd done last night. I'd gone to the Abbey. The last thing I remembered was being there, breaking down into uncontrollable sobs, and falling asleep. At what point did I get up and come home?

A soft knock rapped against the door.

My breath caught in my throat. Was it Sophie? "Hello?" I said, my voice cracking.

The door opened and when Luke's handsome face popped through the gap, I breathed a sigh of relief.

"Morning," he said, giving me a warm smile.

"Hey," I said, offering the best smile I could in return. "You can come in. I'm decent."

He slid through the half open door, then closed it behind him. "How are you feeling?"

A dull throb had started in the back of my skull, my eyes felt sore and puffy, and my stomach grumbled. I hadn't eaten at all yesterday.

"I'm ok," I said, sitting up. "What are you doing here?"

"I…I kind of found you…last night…at the Abbey. I brought you home."

I gasped. How embarrassing. He'd found me? In the middle of the field, distraught because my vampire boyfriend had abandoned me at the most crucial point in my life?

"Oh my…I'm so sorry," I whispered. "I never meant to…" I swallowed the lump in my throat. "I don't know what happened."

"It's ok. The main thing is you're safe."

"Thanks…for bringing me home."

"No need to thank me. Is there anything I can get you? A drink, some breakfast?"

My tummy rumbled, reminding me it was empty, but the upsetting mix of simmering fury and despair squashed my appetite right down. I didn't feel like doing anything.

I shook my head. "No, thank you."

He gave me a look, one of 'you should know better', and said, "Are you sure?"

I hesitated for the slightest of moments. "Yes, thank you. I think I just want to sleep…"

I wanted to sleep to ignore the pain, hide from the aching chasm yawning deep inside me, growing wider and more profound with every second I stayed awake.

"Well, I have some things to finish off outside so I'll be around most of the day. If you need me, just yell, ok? Don't forget your mum and Hannah will be here at lunchtime."

"What time is it?"

"A little after eight."

"You don't have to work today, Luke."

He chuckled. "Honestly, it's ok. Besides, I've got some other things lined up for the next few days so if I don't get finished up today, I don't know when I can get them done."

I waved a hand through the air dismissively. "Whenever is fine. There's no rush."

"Look," he said, lowering his voice. "If I'm being honest, I don't want to leave you alone today."

"I won't be alone. Sophie and Joanna will be wandering around somewhere."

As I said Joanna's name, I remembered the whole mess with the witches. More fury rose inside me and I found myself gritting my teeth.

"Don't say anything," Luke said, lowering his voice. "You need to play this clever, Cat."

"They tricked me into killing my dad," I said, scrunching up the duvet. "You've no idea what I'm feeling right now."

"I think I have a good idea. Don't let your emotions get the better of you. At the moment, you have the upper hand. Don't lose it."

I squeezed my eyes shut and counted to ten, then let out a long breath. "I'm not sure I can keep my mouth shut, Luke."

"Maybe it's a good thing if I stick around then."

I nodded. "I'm not going to argue with that."

"How about we clear your head for the morning before your mum arrives? Keep you out of the way of Joanna?"

"What do you have in mind?"

"Riding, of course."

I jumped out of bed like a spring chicken. "Ok, let's go."

He chuckled and held the door open for me. I trotted down the stairs, managing a smile at least, until I heard the twins giggling in the kitchen. I stopped on the first-floor landing and looked at Luke.

"It's ok," he said. "You got this."

I shook my head. "No, I don't. I want to kill her."

"Cat, remember what I said."

I took a deep breath and counted to twenty. By the time I let it out, I felt no different. Not in the slightest. If anything, her cheery voice did nothing but irritate me more.

"Do I need to kiss you again to distract you?"

I rolled my eyes and gave him a withering look. "No."

He gestured towards the stairs. "Then let's move."

"I'm going to downgrade you to pal again if you're not careful."

He chuckled. "So long as you're doing the right thing, I couldn't care less. Put me in a skirt and call me

Linda if you like, hell I'll even wear high heels."

"That might be a sight to see actually."

"You're braver than me then."

I giggled but as we hit the bottom step and I saw my Dad's closed bedroom door, all traces of happiness vanished. How could I be laughing and joking and debating going for a ride when my dad had died a day ago?

Without thinking, I opened the bedroom door. Joanna was inside, stripping the bed.

"Hey, Cat," she said, her voice soft. "I'm so sorry." She came towards me with her arms outstretched. "He was a lovely man."

Shocked, stunned, I didn't have words to describe how I felt. This was my dad's room, now a sacred space. What the hell was she of all people doing in here?

I stepped back and held my arm out to stop her getting any closer. "What are you doing in here?"

"I thought I'd change the bed," she replied, her eyes filling with unease. She looked at Luke briefly then back at me and said, "I thought I'd make the room nice again so you could spend as much time in here as you wanted."

My anger towards her simmered inside me. I wanted nothing more than to wrap my hands around her skinny little throat and throttle her. "Well don't!" I yelled. "No one told you that you could even come in here. Just because you work here it doesn't mean you have free rein of the place."

"Ok, ok," she said, holding her hands up and backing away from the bed. "I'm sorry. I clearly made a mistake."

Loud banging on the window made me jump. I

looked out to see hail pelting at the windows. The blue sky had turned almost black. I turned back to her and said, "I think you've done that alright. Just get out. Don't ever come in here again! Do you understand?"

She glanced down at the floor and nodded.

"Cat," Luke said, putting a hand on my shoulder. "Calm down."

I whirled around and glared at him. "Like hell I'll calm down. Nobody touches my dad's stuff. Nobody."

"I know, I know," he said, putting his arm around me. He pulled me into his chest and wrapped his big arms around me. "It's all going to be ok."

I burst into tears. I heard Joanna run past him, her shoes clicking on the wooden floor. The twins had fallen silent and almost immediately, a wave of guilt hit me. Luke shut the door behind us and just held me.

After a few minutes I pulled back and said, "I feel so bad. I should apologise to her, shouldn't I?"

"Don't do anything whilst your emotions are running wild. Emotional decisions are never good ones."

I sighed and looked at the pouring rain. "Doesn't look like we'll be going riding after all."

"How about we sit and watch some Midsummer Murders until your mum gets here?"

"Sure, ok." As I looked at Dad's bed, the sheets half off thanks to Joanna, I remembered our last conversation. "Wait." I ran over to the bookcase. "Dad said there's a safe behind here. There's something in it that I need."

"Cat, I put those bookcases there. There is no safe there."

"He told me there was a safe behind here with all his family journals in. I need them, Luke. I need my magic, it's the only way I'm going to beat those witches."

I went to one end of the huge bookcase and motioned with my head for him to go to the other. "Please, Luke. Will you just help me move this?"

He came over and told me to move. As quick as I opened my mouth to protest, I shut it again. In the blink of an eye, he'd moved the entire thing with minimal effort, like he was moving nothing but a chair at most.

I scanned my eyes over the flowery wallpaper, looking for anything out of the ordinary. In the very bottom left corner, where one wall met with the other, I spotted something that didn't look quite right.

"Can you move this a little further out please?" I said, squeezing myself between the bookcase and the wall.

Luke obliged, creating enough room for him to follow me down.

"There," I said, pointing at the bottom corner. "The wallpaper is sticking out."

He peered over my shoulder. "Looks flat to me."

"Do you need your eyes testing?"

"I can see nearly two miles away in the dark, Caitlyn. No."

I shrugged my shoulders. "Just because they work in the dark, doesn't mean they do in daylight."

He said nothing, making me smirk. I could just picture the frown on his face however I didn't want to take my eyes off the wallpaper mound. I knelt down and brushed my hand over it, feeling something solid underneath.

"Bingo," I said, ripping at the wallpaper. "He's papered over the safe."

"What are you doing?"

"Getting to the safe."

"No, Cat, you're ripping wallpaper. Are you ok? When did you last eat or drink?"

I ignored him and carried on, eventually ripping my way through the paper to a small black safe. I became totally confused then as it had no visible way of opening it. No keypad for numbers, no dial either, not even a handle. I pressed my palm against it, wondering if it was a door you had to push in to get it to pop open. Nothing.

"Cat, I'm starting to get a bit worried now. I think I need to get you out of here."

"It's here, Luke, how can you not see it?"

"Ok," he said. "I'm calling time. Enough." He put his hand on my shoulder and then froze. "Oh."

"Do you see it now?"

"Yes, sorry, Cat."

"You can grovel later. First I need to get into the damn thing."

"Let me have a look," he said, bending down next to me. He removed his hand from me to support himself. "It's gone."

I frowned. "No, it's right there."

He put his hand back on my shoulder. "Yes. Huh. Seems I can only see it if I'm touching you."

"That makes me think it's linked to the family somehow. Maybe through blood?"

"If there's one thing I know about witches, it's that their gut instinct is half their power."

I didn't have time to ponder over that thought too much but the mention of blood did make me think twice about how to open it. I carefully pressed all my fingertips against every inch of the front of it. As I neared the right-hand edge, a sharp prick on my index finger made me jump back. I looked at my finger to see a drop of rose red blood sitting on my fingertip.

When the door swung open, I quickly forgot about my bleeding finger and looked inside the safe. I expected it to be small; the door couldn't have been much bigger than a standard sized book, but as I peered in, it seemed to be nothing short of a tardis. Photos, newspaper clippings, a pair of shoes, a necklace, cufflinks, money, and at the back, a stack of brown leather journals.

"Hey," I said, looking back at Luke. "You should check this out."

He knelt down alongside me and looked inside. "Wow. That's pretty cool."

"Do you think you can reach the journals at the back?"

"I'm not sure but I'll give it a go." He stuck his hand inside, then brought it back out, cursing.

"What's wrong?"

"That is searing hot in there. Like an incinerator."

"Are you ok?" I said, turning his hand over. Angry red blisters covered his hand, the skin seared off most of them. "Let me get some ice."

"It's ok," he said, wiggling his fingers. "I'm healing."

I watched in amazement as his burned skin quickly disappeared under the cover of new skin, leaving no trace of any injury whatsoever. "Now that's cool."

He grinned. "I'll agree with you there."

I eyed up the safe with suspicion, wondering if there was some sort of booby trap.

"Don't," he said. "You won't heal like me."

I shook my head. "I think it's blood specific. Only one way to find out." I thrust my hand inside and squeezed my eyes shut. After a couple of seconds, I let out the breath I didn't realise I'd been holding. "I'm ok."

"You are literally going to give me a heart attack one day."

I grinned and silently wished I had a longer arm so I could reach the damn journals. Literally, as I thought that, my open hand filled with the smooth leather of the journal covers.

"I've got them," I said, pulling them out as fast as I could.

All five of them fell onto the floor together with a cloud of dust. The brown leather had faded and cracked in places, making them look like they belonged in some sort of museum. I picked up the one on top and undid the leather string keeping the covers closed.

The pages crinkled and rustled as I flicked through them, sending a shiver down my spine. I stopped close to the front and decided to read something. The page I chose showed how to release someone's memories. It depicted an ingredients list for a potion, but also a spell that could be cast over a sleeping person.

I looked up at Luke and grinned. "This is where the fun starts."

CHAPTER TWENTY-THREE

We didn't watch any Midsummer Murders. We sat at Dad's desk and scoured through the journals. I knew exactly what I was looking for—the spell to unbind my magic. After scrutinising two of them, I still hadn't found what I wanted.

"Hey, look at this," I said, nudging Luke and pointing to the current open page.

He took one look at it and widened his eyes in fright. "I actually thought you were joking."

"I kind of was," I said, giggling. "I made that up about Joanna, but it looks like someone has actually turned male genitals green."

"Someone in your bloodline," he said, moving his chair away from me.

I laughed. "Calm down. You've not upset me that much. Yet."

He gave me a nervous look from the corner of his

eye and continued looking through the journal in front of him. "As fascinating as it is looking through old witch diaries, it would be helpful if you told me what you were looking for."

I sighed. "You have to promise not to get mad."

He narrowed his eyes. "That means it's stupid and you know it." I cleared my throat and pushed my journal towards him, still open on the page for green genitals. "Alright, fine. I won't get mad."

I shook my head. "Say 'I promise'."

He sighed and rolled his eyes. "I promise I won't get mad," he said, his tone nothing but sarcastic.

"I'm looking for a spell to unbind my magic."

He opened his mouth then immediately closed it. His whiskey brown eyes filled with nothing but worry.

"I have to, Luke. I need to release my mum's memories. And considering what I'm up against, I can't afford to have a disadvantage."

Letting out a long breath, he said, "Maybe you should release your mum's memories first. Then you'll have a better idea of what it is you're up against."

"I can't do that without magic."

"I'll shut up then," he said, chuckling.

"The witches, one in particular, wants my power. If I don't comply with her, she'll kill me and take it anyway."

He snorted. "Like hell she'll even get close enough to kill you."

"I appreciate the gesture, Luke, but she's powerful. Dad called her a demon."

Curiosity flooded his eyes. "What's her name?"

"Keres."

He scrubbed his hands over his face. "That's the one name I didn't want you to say. Remember I said I knew who the crazy old lady was? That's her."

I shook my head. "It's not. They look nothing alike."

"You don't think she could change her outward appearance?"

My heart skipped a beat. "Then I have even more reason to unbind my magic. Didn't you say something about Gordon being hired by her?"

He nodded. "I would bet my last penny that she's hired Gordon to follow you. If you don't bend to her will, she'll use him to get what she needs."

"But he can't hurt me, he's related to Marcus."

Luke smiled. "What he forgot to detail was that Gordon can hurt you, he just can't kill you."

My throat ran dry and my heart started pounding. "Wait, what?"

"He can take your blood without killing you."

I started shaking. I hadn't expected this. Knowing Gordon was out there, lurking in the shadows, watching my every move, it filled me with fear. A ball of nausea knotted together in my stomach.

"Hey," Luke said, reaching across the desk and taking my hand. "It's ok. He'll have to get through me first and that is not going to happen."

I smiled, trying to ignore the cloak of comfort soothing my soul. "I'd hate if you got hurt because of me, Luke. This isn't your battle."

His entire face changed, softening and filling with warmth and reassurance. The look in his eyes took my breath away. I'd heard that eyes were the window to the soul and right in that moment, I could see straight into Luke's. The love and adoration pouring from them rooted me to the spot. No one had ever looked at me like that.

"You know how I feel about you, Caitlyn. You may not want this to be my battle, but it already is."

I tried to think of something to say but all of a sudden my chest felt tight and no matter how much air I tried to breathe in, it became tighter and tighter, like someone had put a vice around me. My mind raced at a million miles an hour, trying to make sense of all this but I didn't know what pieces went where. It was just too much.

"Hey," Luke said, putting one of his hands on my back. "Calm down. Just take one deep breath in, hold it for a second, and then let it out."

I did as he said, breathing in and breathing out when he prompted. After a few minutes, the tightness in my chest loosened. I felt absolutely exhausted and totally drained.

"What was that?" I breathed.

"A panic attack."

I put my face in my hands and shook my head. "Great," I said, moving my hands. "That's all I need right now. Having a pathetic panic attack right when I need to be doing the exact opposite."

"They're not pathetic, Cat. It's your body's way of telling you it's stressed. You've got so much on your shoulders right now it's a wonder it's not happened before."

I stabbed a finger at the open page of the journal. "Which is exactly why I need to unbind my magic. It'll give me strength when I think I don't have any."

Luke pressed his lips together and sighed. "Ok. I'm not going to fight you on it. I'll help you find it."

I reached over and grabbed his hand. "Thank you. I really don't know where I'd be right now if you weren't here."

"No need to thank me," he said. "It's my pleasure."

I gave him a warm smile and turned my attention back to the journals.

***

Just over an hour later, Luke found exactly what I needed in the very last journal.

"I think this is it," he said, pushing the old diary over the desk towards me.

On the left-hand page was a spell detailing how to bind someone's magic. On the right-hand page, the spell to unbind. The writing was old and faded in parts but written in a captivating italic scrawl I couldn't stop staring at. I traced my fingers over the ink and as I did, flashes of a man with a quill, scribbling away under candlelight flooded my mind.

"Wow," I said. "I think I just saw who wrote this."

Luke's eyes brightened with wonder. "Really?"

I chewed my lip as I thought of something. "Hey, let me try something. Give me your hand."

He put his hand out on the desk, palm down, and I placed my right hand on top of it. With my left hand, I touched the ink once again, more images of the man unfolding in my mind. This time he scurried through narrow passageways of a castle, carrying one candle that barely had anything left to it. The journal was tucked underneath his arm and he kept looking behind him, his blue eyes full of fear.

"Do you see it?" I asked him.

Even before he answered, I knew his reply. His eyes, widened in shock, were also slightly glazed over, as if he were daydreaming and not really paying attention.

"Yes," he breathed. "That's fascinating."

I nodded. "I wonder if I'll get more once I unbind myself?"

"I don't think there's any question of that," he said.

I broke our connection and looked at the two spells. I had expected the unbinding spell to be a reversal of the binding spell and it seemed my assumption had been correct.

The binding spell required a long list of ingredients including seven red ribbons tied into a bow, seven spiders plucked from their webs, seven live snakes, and worryingly, a cup of my blood.

I turned my left palm over and looked at the long white scar running diagonally from my index finger to the bottom of my hand. My understanding of that injury was that I'd tripped and fallen on a glass pane as a toddler. Now, I knew exactly where I'd acquired it from.

"Look at this," Luke said, pointing to the list of ingredients for the unbinding spell. It listed one ingredient only.

All of the original potion used to bind the witch

I frowned. "What? I have no idea where it even is. And I can't release Mum's memories without unbinding myself."

Scouring down the steps of the binding spell, I found the answer to my potion's whereabouts in the very last step.

Place the potion into a glass vial. Seal with a cork kissed by a fire siren. Secure in a dark place never visited.

I sighed. "Where the hell is that?"

"Do you think it's in the safe?"

"I doubt it, but I can look."

I headed over to the safe. Of course, the door had shut itself which meant I needed to give up some more of my precious blood to reopen it. After being pricked in exactly the same place as before, I silently cursed the stupid thing as I peered inside.

What made this even harder was the fact that all I knew was to look for something in glass. I presumed it would be liquid considering it had to be brewed in salt water but with all the other weird ingredients, it could well have been something as peculiar as neon coloured sand.

"I don't think there's anything in here," I said, shutting the safe door and sighing.

"Witch spells are very specific in their wording," Luke said. "It says 'a dark place never visited'. That insinuates to me that you could go there, but no one does."

I walked back to the desk and plonked myself down in the chair. "That could be a million and one places, Luke. Along with the dead snakes and spiders and all those herbs and things, it's too complicated anyway."

"Maybe your mum will know?"

I smiled. "You mean in the memories she doesn't remember?"

Luke chuckled. "Yep, that'll be the one. The memories she can't remember until you unbind your magic."

I sighed and leaned my head back on the chair, looking up at the ceiling. "I need a break."

"That's good," he said. "Because your mum has just arrived.

CHAPTER TWENTY-FOUR

"Kitty Cat," Mum said, throwing herself at me and encasing me in the worlds most painful hug. "I'm so sorry."

Mum had always been slim but in the four months I'd not seen her, she'd lost weight. Her idea of a hug involved squeezing the life out of someone which wasn't normally a problem, but I could feel her bones, even through her clothes.

"Are you ok?" I asked, peeling her off me. "You've lost a lot of weight."

She batted her hand through the air and tutted. "I'm fine. I've been doing yoga twice a day."

My mind had hurtled to the worst conclusion already—cancer. Was she possibly hiding something from me? "Mum, if you're sick, you need to tell me."

She grabbed me by the arms, her fingers digging into my flesh, and looked me square in the eye. "I'm as healthy as a horse."

I said no more. Luke stood patiently behind me, so I said, "Mum, I'd like you to meet—"

"Marcus," she said, rushing forwards and grabbing Luke's hand. "I've heard so much about you, mostly from Hannah on the drive up here because Kitty Cat doesn't like talking about boys to me." She grinned and then her entire face flushed red. "But of course, you're no boy, I can tell you're all man."

"MUM!" I wanted the ground to open up and swallow me right about now.

Luke smiled and patted Mum's hand. "My name is Luke Freeman. We spoke on the phone."

Mum slapped a hand over her mouth as her entire face turned beetroot red. "I'm so sorry." Then she looked at me and playfully slapped my arm. "Kitty Cat, why didn't you stop me before I opened my mouth?"

I rolled my eyes and glanced at Hannah, who, bless her heart, had stood with her back pressed against the front door the entire time, not saying a word. She came at me with her arms outstretched and gave me one of her signature hugs. She gave absolutely world class friend hugs. I closed my eyes and enjoyed the moment.

"You didn't tell me you had two hunks in your life," she whispered in my ear.

I couldn't help but giggle. Typical Hannah to ease the tension with a joke. I opened my eyes and stepped back, catching sight of a playful smile tweaking at Luke's lips. He'd heard her. Could this get any more embarrassing?

"Would you like some help with your bags?" Luke said, gesturing towards the door.

"Oh," Mum said, gushing like a teenage girl with

her first crush. "And such a gentleman too. Are you single?"

"MUM! Seriously?"

She looked at me and grinned. "Bet you've missed me, hey, Kitty Cat?"

Luke opened the front door and headed outside to the car, shadowed by Mum.

"Like a hole in the head," I said, looking at Hannah. "Thank you for enduring hours confined in a small space with her."

"Anything for my bestie," she replied. "Besides, I need to meet Marcus. Where is he?"

I pulled my lips into a thin line. "Yeah, he's not here. He's gone away for a few days."

Hannah's jaw dropped. "You are kidding me, right? He left you whilst all this was going on?"

I sighed. "Believe me, I'm not happy, but it's to do with his missing mum."

"This might sound a little harsh, but she'll still be missing tomorrow, the day after, and even next week. He couldn't have delayed it for a few days?"

In my mind, I'd already justified it. Marcus needed to find those witches and solve the riddle of his mum. He'd been in emotional agony for two centuries. My pain would still be here when he got back. Deep down though, real deep down, I knew what Hannah was saying was correct. He should have been here.

"It was one of those leads where he had to follow it up straight away or risk losing it."

Hannah frowned. "Ok, whatever. Let's talk about hunk number two. Where did you find him?"

"He's dad's handyman."

"No way. You get to see him every day?" She raised her eyebrows. "Can I come live with you?"

"What about Daniel?" I asked, referring to her current beau. They'd been going steady for nearly a year.

"Who?" she replied. "Daniel who?"

"Have you split up again?"

She shook her head. "How can you even mention his name? It's like comparing fatty burnt bacon to a prime cut of steak that just melts in the mouth."

"Hannah
," I said, laughing.

"Look at him," she said, cocking her head to one side and admiring the view of Luke. "Makes me realise I need to be looking at men, not boys."

As Luke hauled four suitcases out of the boot of the car, Mum actually went up to him and stroked his arm, asking if he needed help.

"I think I might be burying both of my parents at this rate," I said.

***

After Luke dragged their overloaded suitcases onto the first floor and showed them their respective rooms, he came back down to me in Dad's room.

"Interesting mum you have there, Kitty Cat," he said, chuckling.

"I hate that name. She's called me it since I was three."

"I think it's cute."

"You're hardly going to disagree with a woman who's literally just drooled all over you, are you?"

Luke sat down next to me. He leaned over and said, "Why? Are you jealous?"

"No," I said, maybe a little too quickly. "It's just

wrong. You're my friend and she's my mum. It's weird."

"I quite like jealousy on you, looks cute."

I slammed the journal I was reading shut and fixed him a steely stare. "Jealousy is wanting something someone else has. Protecting what's mine is being territorial. Get it right."

He quirked an eyebrow up. "I'm yours now, am I?"

I faltered for a second. I hadn't even realised what I'd just said. "Yes, you're my friend. A good friend at that."

He smiled. "As your good friend, I can assure you I have no romantic interest in your mum."

"Or Hannah?"

"Or Hannah. My brother might be quite taken with her though."

"I am not introducing her to Mason, she doesn't deserve that punishment. Mum on the other hand…"

Luke chuckled. "No, not Mason. You've not met him, but you'd get on great. His name is Max."

I smirked. "Oh yes…that infamous M again."

He narrowed his eyes at me. "Don't you dare."

"Don't you think it'd be fun to see what Mum thinks of it?"

"No, I really really don't."

"Spoil sport."

He gave me a cheeky wink then said, "Your mum would probably think it's rather cute. Shall we test the theory?"

He had a point there. She would most likely say it was adorable and dribble all over him even more. "Ok, you win. No more mention of the M word."

"Thought as much."

"You don't play fair."

"I didn't realise I had to?"

I laughed. "Well yes. You have to let me win. All the time."

"And that's playing fair, is it?"

"Duh."

He laughed. "Ok. I'll see what I can do but no promises."

Hannah came in then, asking for food.

"You and your stomach," I said, standing up. "I'm telling you, you've got worms. No one eats as much as you do and doesn't gain weight."

"I have a high metabolism, it's not my fault. I was born this way."

I rolled my eyes. "Yeah, like I've not heard that one before."

As I took Hannah into the kitchen, Mum came downstairs and followed us. I popped some crumpets in the toaster, mindful of not making too much mess before Sophie had to prepare tea. She hated a cluttered kitchen.

"You've not forgotten how I like mine, have you?" Hannah said.

"No, Hannah," I said, getting the knife and the butter out.

For some weird reason, she liked the top and the bottom buttered. It didn't matter how many times I told her the butter dripped through to the bottom anyway, she wouldn't have it.

"But you only butter one side of toast," I'd say. "Or butter one side of the bread for a sandwich."

"Yes, but this isn't toast or a sandwich, is it? It's mine, which means I can eat it how I like."

It was a constant argument we'd had for years. I

wasn't feeling particularly playful at the moment though to poke fun at it.

"What time did you guys set off?" I asked, plonking down a plate with eight crumpets on.

"Hannah stayed at mine last night and we left around four this morning."

"I wondered if you'd come early. Luke said you'd be here at dinner time."

"I needed to be here as soon as possible for my little girl," Mum said, in between mouthfuls of crumpets.

"Thanks, Mum."

"Do you want to talk about it?"

I shook my head, tears instantly springing from nowhere. "Not right now, no."

"Is there anything you want to talk about?"

The toasters popped up at the same time, another eight crumpets done. Of course there was something I wanted to talk about, I just hadn't figured out yet how to broach the subject.

"Actually, yes," I said, turning my back on her as I took all the crumpets out. "But perhaps now isn't the best of times."

"No time like the present," Mum said.

"That's true," I said, smearing butter all over Hannah's four crumpets.

"Especially when you have that bitch Keres on your tail."

The knife in my hand clattered to the floor. I turned around, shaking, and leaned back on the worktop to support myself. My heart pounded so hard I could hear my own pulse.

"What did you just say?"

Luke strode into the kitchen and came straight to

my side. He bent down and picked up the knife. Then he turned to Hannah and said, "You are, aren't you?"

She crossed her legs at her ankles and leaned back in her chair, really pulling off the whole nonchalant vibe. Biting into a butter dripping crumpet, she grinned and said, "Yep."

"What?" I asked.

Mum stood up and walked over to me, putting her hands on my shoulders. "Hannah gave me a potion last night, Kitty Cat. I remember everything."

CHAPTER TWENTY-FIVE

I froze for a few minutes because I didn't know what to say or do. Hannah was something, I guessed a witch from the whole potion comment, and my mum had all her memories back. I certainly hadn't expected this.

"Are you ok?" Luke said, rubbing his hand on my back.

"Are you a witch?" I asked Hannah.

She shook her head. "Nope. I'm something you would never expect."

I glanced at Luke.

"Hannah is a gargoyle," he said, as if it was the most natural thing to say.

"A what? As in the ugly stone creatures that sit on a church?"

"Uh hum," Hannah said, coughing. "Do I look like an ugly stone creature to you?"

Luke laughed. "Gargoyles are classed as shifters

because they shift from human form to their…not so human form."

"Do I dare ask what that might be?" I asked, looking at Hannah with a raised eyebrow.

"We don't turn into stone, but we do have exceptionally thick skin. Not much can penetrate it."

"But what do you look like? Are you…you?"

Hannah grinned. "Oh no. We kind of look like trolls to be honest."

"You mean like full on naked and slimy and stuff?"

She laughed. "No, there's no slime, thank you very much."

"But you are naked?"

"Not as me, in human form, but naked in the sense that gargoyles don't really have genitals so there's nothing to cover."

I frowned. "But if you don't have genitals then how do you…you know…make more of you?"

"You mean HAVE SEX?"

My entire face flushed with heat. I don't know why, I just couldn't bring myself to say the word. It felt naughty for some reason.

"Our Cat here has a really bad aversion to the word SEX, don't you, Cat?" Hannah said, grinning like a Cheshire cat.

Luke put his arm around my shoulder and squeezed me. "I think it's cute."

"I'm certainly not complaining," Mum said.

"Alright, alright. Can we please stop trying to embarrass me?"

Hannah laughed. "In answer to your question, we have to be in human form to reproduce."

I pointed at her. "Now that word I can deal with."

I pursed my lips and asked, "Have you known about me all this time?"

She nodded. "Think of us as bodyguards. I was born specifically with the purpose of being your bodyguard, so I had an extra shot of magic most gargoyles don't get. That means I'm stronger, fiercer, and tougher than a regular gargoyle."

I didn't know what to say. How could I possibly even begin to process that? Did this mean our entire friendship had been nothing but a lie? Something that was forced rather than something that developed naturally?

"Are you ok, Kitty Cat?" Mum asked. "You've gone a little pale."

I nodded. "Yeah…it's just a bit of a shock. I didn't expect to find out that my best friend was actually forced to be my best friend." A wave of tears built up in my eyes, springing out of nowhere. "I need some air."

My mind swimming with emotions and trying to make sense of everything, I ran for the back door and opened it, only to reveal the beginning of yet another rain shower. I slammed the door shut and sighed, cursing the stupid weather and everything about this whole damn scenario.

"Kitty Cat," Mum said, walking into the utility room. "I know it's a lot to take in but it's going to be alright now."

Mum put her hand on my back. Leaning against the worktop over the washing machine, I stared at the black marble effect, trying to make patterns out of the silver specks. I knew she was trying to comfort me, but I just wanted to be on my own to process all of this at my own speed, chunk by morbid chunk.

"My whole life is unravelling around me, Mum," I said, still staring at the worktop. "I've been encased in layers of lies for eighteen years and now all those layers are being peeled away and I feel nothing but naked, vulnerable, exposed. I don't even know who I am anymore."

"You're still you, Caitlyn," she said. I knew when she used my real name she was being serious. "You always will be you. No one can take that away from you."

I turned around and sighed. "But who is Caitlyn Summers? I thought a week ago I was a regular eighteen-year-old girl with a vampire boyfriend. Now I'm some doppelganger nuclear bomb of a witch who everyone apparently wants a piece of. My parents aren't human, my best friend isn't either, and I've been abandoned by said vampire boyfriend and left in the care of a werewolf. I mean, what is this?"

"It's your life, sweetpea," she said, her emerald green eyes full of love and care.

"It wasn't my life a week ago, a month ago, heck, six months ago I didn't even know vampires were real."

"It's ok to feel like this. It's perfectly understandable and expected. Just take it all in at your own pace."

I folded my arms over my chest and in my most sarcastic voice said, "But not too long because things need doing, right?"

Mum looked at the floor. I didn't want her to feel bad but to some degree I kind of wanted her to. I felt trapped and totally isolated, I didn't know what to think, say, or even feel.

"I need to get and out do something," I said,

sighing. "Luke, can we still go riding please? I need to clear my head."

He plodded through and looked out of the window in the utility room. "It's raining, but sure."

"Can we go for a drive then or something? I just can't stay in here."

"Of course. Let me go sort a couple of things and then we'll go."

I nodded, feeling like a mountain had just been lifted from my shoulders. "I'm sorry, Mum. I know you've only just got here but I just…it's too much for me at the minute."

Mum nodded and grabbed my hand. "It's fine. Hannah and I can stay here and formulate plans on what to do next. We need to make sure the funeral is security tight."

The funeral. I hadn't even thought about the funeral yet. A wave of nausea rolled through my stomach. All of a sudden, my chest felt tight, the same constricting feeling from yesterday. The more I tried to suck in air, the tighter my chest became. I felt trapped in my own body and my own mind. I wanted to scream to free myself, but I could barely breathe enough air to keep myself alive. My brain kicked into survival mode, demanding more air but my body refused to cooperate.

Panic and fear hit me like a sledgehammer. Was this it? Was I going to suffocate myself to death? The more I tried to rid myself of such a claustrophobic feeling, the more I felt stuck and helpless. Tears rolled down my cheeks and I looked at Mum through a hazy film of water. Her eyes were flooded with terror and she yelled for Luke. Everything seemed to move in slow motion and I wondered if this was what happened when you were about to die. Is this what Dad experienced? Or did he see a bright light and walk towards it, engulfing himself in the afterlife forever? Did his life flash before his eyes, in his dreams? Had he woken up to try to tell me a final goodbye, only to find me asleep?

Luke ran through the kitchen and into the utility room. He stood in front of me and put his hands on my shoulders. "Cat, Cat, look at me."

I managed to move my eyes just enough to stare into his whiskey brown depths. Full of worry and concern, a pang of guilt hit my heart. I could see the profoundness of his feelings for me reflecting back at me.

"Cat, calm down and breathe with me," he said. "Hold your breath, now breathe out. Good. Breathe in, hold it, now breathe out."

He continued instructing me for a minute or so until the vice like grip on my chest started loosening. I couldn't help but feel like a lucky mouse who'd escaped an invisible anaconda. A few minutes later, my breathing returned to normal, except for the wall of tiredness that suddenly hit me like a wrecking ball.

"Are you ok?" Luke said, rubbing his hands up and down my arms.

I nodded. "I'm tired."

"Let's get you to bed," he said, slipping an arm around my shoulders and ushering me through into the kitchen.

"Do you need anything, Cat?" Mum asked, her voice shaking.

I shook my head. "I just need to sleep for an hour or so."

"I'm not going anywhere. None of us are. We'll be right here when you wake up."

"Thank you," I said.

Luke guided me into the hallway and to the stairs. When I put my right foot on the bottom step and put my weight on my leg, my leg started shaking and I fell to my knees.

"Ok, that's enough," he said, scooping me up like a feather. "Do you want me to stay with you?"

I rested my head against his chest and nodded.

A sharp knock at the front door made me jump, sending my heart into supersonic speeds.

"It's just the postman," Luke said, putting me carefully down on the stairs. "Two seconds."

Luke opened the door and took a parcel. A long slender box wrapped in lilac coloured paper had me questioning what on earth it was.

"It looks like this is for you," Luke said, handing me the mysterious item.

I didn't have the energy to query it. I took it from him and turned it over, spotting the address label with my name on it. In beautiful italic handwriting. Marcus' handwriting.

I glanced up at Luke, my entire body trembling. "It's from Marcus."

Luke's eyes flickered towards the kitchen. "Just a parcel for Cat," he shouted. "It's all sorted."

"Ok," Mum called back.

Luke walked back up to me and picked me up. "You're not opening that down here," he whispered.

He carried me up to bed, laid me down, then closed and locked the door. When he came back to the bed, I was laid on my side, staring at the parcel.

"You going to open it?"

I sighed. "I'm nervous to."

"Do you want me to open it?"

He laid down on his side, mirroring me. I pushed it across the bed towards him. He'd left a fair amount of space in between us.

In a matter of seconds, he'd shredded the pretty paper to reveal a dark blue velvet box. My heart jumped instantly. I knew it was jewellery.

Luke opened the lid, his eyes instantly widening. "I dread to think what that cost," he said. "And it looks like you've got a note." He picked up a folded piece of paper and handed it to me as he turned the box around.

When I caught sight of what had surprised him so much, I gasped. A diamond encrusted necklace complete with a silver clasped moonstone in a drop pendant stared back at me. With my birthday being in June, I had a choice of three stones for my birth month. Moonstone had always been the one for me.

I opened the note to see more of his familiar handwriting which read,

My darling Caitlyn, I know I am not there to ease the pain of your father's untimely passing but please take comfort in this reminder of me. I kissed each stone before sending it to you. I will return home soon. My longing to be with you is my greatest desire right now. All my love, Marcus.

I read the note several times. I didn't really know what to make of it. Not only that, I didn't have the energy to think about it nor discuss it right now.

"Can you put it on the floor please?" I said, closing the lid and pushing it back to Luke. "I can't deal with that right now." I threw the note at him and said, "Make of that what you will."

He put the box on the floor, before reading the note. When he'd finished, he raised an eyebrow. "Let's not deal with that right now."

I nodded. "Sleep first."

He closed his eyes and folded his arms over his chest, appearing to be peacefully asleep almost instantly. I studied his face for several minutes, wondering why his handsomeness had never struck me in the same way Marcus' did.

His long dark eyelashes rested against his bronzed cheeks, his skin smooth like velvet. Finger length brown hair gleamed like smoky quartz and his clothes clung to his lithe body. He was always warm, always smiling, always knew how to put me at ease. I realised he was ruggedly handsome, a proper working man who would still be just as handsome at sixty years of age.

Yet Marcus, who resembled nothing short of a Calvin Klein poster model, was handsome in a completely different way. He was simply breath taking to look at, but had he been human, his good looks would have worn away by the time he was forty. However, he wasn't even vaguely human.

I sighed. Marcus had lived a long time. He was refined, sophisticated, meticulous with everything he did. The way he moved, the way he spoke, the way he handled different situations and different people was so smooth, like a well-rehearsed actor in front of a camera. He lived a life three levels up from mine and it fascinated me. I was like a magpie being dazzled with shiny things and promises.

Being in his world made me feel like I'd made it into some secret society but no matter where he took me or what beautiful necklace he bought me, he never quite touched me emotionally, spiritually, not like Luke did.

That was the first time I began to question me and Marcus seriously. The whole ex thing aside, where were we going anyway? He lied to me and left me alone in the middle of the night, abandoned me when I needed him the most. Being with Marcus would ensure a life of drama, passionate arguments, and missing elements of things I wanted and needed.

But I couldn't deny the fact I loved him. Or was it in fact lust? As much as I was mad at him right now, I knew I had feelings for him that were unresolved, even if they were in question.

I sighed and closed my eyes. Everything was always better after a sleep.

CHAPTER TWENTY-SIX

When I woke, I felt like I'd had a battery recharge. It seemed like I'd had a perspective alteration just by going to sleep.

"How are you feeling?"

Staring at my polka dot socks, trying to count the white dots, as I mused in my thoughts, I hadn't even looked at Luke yet.

I lifted my head and smiled. "I feel a lot better, thank you."

"You seem more relaxed."

I nodded. "I do feel a little guilty though."

"About what?"

"Hannah."

"Ah."

I frowned. "What do you mean 'ah'?"

"I know she was upset that you thought she'd been forced to be your best friend. She wasn't forced to do anything, Cat. She could have hung around in the background of your life. There was no need for her to become your friend in order to protect you."

I pursed my lips. "I figured. I feel awful."

"She'll understand. She's not stupid by any stretch of the imagination."

I quirked an eyebrow up. "Does someone have a soft spot for Hannah?"

He chuckled. "No. I just have a great amount of respect for her kind. They don't have an easy life."

"How do you mean?"

"The witches control them to the extent that only certain bloodlines are allowed to reproduce. They can't have children unless the witches either permit it or demand it. Think of them like guard dogs and the witches being their handlers. They're constantly restrained in some way."

"That's not fair."

"The witches justify it as protecting our entire world. No one has ever dared go against them. They feel that if gargoyles were left to reproduce at will, we would be overrun with bad tempered, difficult to control bulldozers who have the ability to flatten a village with a single shout. So they curb them. Unless required otherwise."

I sat up, my interest piqued and anger starting to simmer in my veins. "So vampires can run around, born and made, drinking witch blood or human blood as they please. Witches can perform some weird form of euthanasia, you wolves can do as you please I'm guessing, but gargoyles are collared and kept? How is that fair?"

"There is no 'fair' in our world, Cat. It is what it is and that's that."

"That says to me that the witches are scared of the gargoyles. They restrain them because they're frightened of their abilities."

Luke's lips tweaked up into a smile. "Have you seen X-Men?"

I frowned. "What?"

"The films, with the mutants, Charles Xavier, Wolverine et cetera."

I rolled my eyes. "I know what you meant, Luke. What has that got to do with this?"

"Do you remember Juggernaut?"

"The giant dude who was like a runaway train?"

Luke nodded. "Pretty much what a gargoyle is."

"Oh."

"Now you understand why they keep them restrained?"

"Kind of but it still doesn't seem fair."

"Imagine a teenage Juggernaut, full of mixed-up hormones, and with anger issues."

I nodded. "Ok, point taken. But that doesn't mean they have to restrict them for life. Just until they're a certain age."

Luke nodded and sat up. "Try telling them that."

"I think it's time to go downstairs and make some apologies."

"Perhaps," he said, leaning down the side of the bed. "But maybe you ought to decide what to do with this first."

Luke put the box containing the necklace on the bed in between us. I stared at it and sighed. Did Marcus think he could ease the pain of him leaving by sending me a necklace through the post? And how did he even know my dad had died? We'd not spoken since he left.

An idea sprung to mind. I opened the box and

touched the necklace, resting my fingertips on the stones. I closed my eyes and let out a long breath. Almost instantly, images of Marcus dominated my mind. A narrow, cobbled street, sandy bricked buildings, a small but expensive looking jewellers. Row upon row of rings, necklaces, earrings, and Marcus scrutinising each one. Then an older gentleman, gift wrapping the blue velvet box, and Marcus passing him a piece of paper before leaving the shop, empty handed, but not alone.

I snatched my hand back from the necklace and snapped the lid shut. "Lying toad," I mumbled, getting off the bed.

"What's wrong? Did you see something?"

I went to the window and stared out, admiring the view of the sea. There was something so peaceful and serene about water, it almost lured you in with the promise of never-ending beauty but hid the fact it could kill you in a split second. *Much like a siren*, I thought to myself.

"I saw him buying the necklace," I said, turning around to face Luke. "He didn't 'kiss each stone' like he said, and he didn't even post it himself—he paid the jeweller to post it."

"Oh."

"He's not even bothered calling me. That night you found me at the Abbey, I'd rung him however many times and he's still not called me back. Then he has the cheek to send that?"

"I'm sure there's a good reason why he hasn't called, Cat. Maybe he can't use his phone or has no signal or something?"

I raised an eyebrow. "Really?"

"Just throwing the possibility out there."

"Why are you making excuses for him? You hate the guy."

Luke shrugged his shoulders. "I just don't want you to jump to conclusions and think the worst. That's not going to help your state of mind."

I sighed. "I appreciate that, Luke, I really do. However, I'm starting to think this 'relationship' isn't what I thought it was. I honestly think his only interest in me was the link to his mum."

"I'm sure it wasn't just that, Cat. You're an amazing woman. He'd be a fool to pass up on you."

"He wasn't alone."

"What do you mean?"

"Exactly what I say, Luke. What I saw when I touched the necklace, he was with that bimbo of a siren, Selina."

Luke quirked an eyebrow up. "Selina? The blonde?"

I folded my arms over my chest and narrowed my eyes at him. "Don't tell me you have a thing for her as well."

He laughed. "No, I most definitely do not. She's well known around here. What was he doing with her?"

I shrugged my shoulders. "You tell me."

"Selina has a lot of contacts. It could well be that she is the one who found him this information in the first place. Don't forget a siren is a witch."

"Was a witch."

He shook his head. "Is a witch."

I frowned. "Marcus said 'was'."

"And you're inclined to believe everything he says?"

"That's a cheap shot."

"But a valid point."

I sighed. "How is she still a witch?"

"Like any other. It just happens that her magic doesn't go beyond anything other than water."

I shook my head. "I saw her death when she fell into the sea. She was throwing fireballs at Marcus."

"When she hit the water though, the water would have taken over her body, including her ability to control fire."

I frowned. "In those journals though, it mentioned a fire siren for the binding spell."

Luke nodded. "Selina is a fire siren. Her born ability to control fire is still in her blood. The fact she lives and relies on water means she can't access that magic, but it's still there. After all, water dowses fire."

"We can switch what elements we control? That's interesting…"

"I don't think it's quite that simple, Cat. She was using magic as she hit the water."

"Which is how a siren is created, yes?"

He nodded.

"And there are thousands of them. Hardly a rare occurrence."

"What are you thinking? I'm not sure I like where this going."

"If you could recreate that energy overtaking the witch as she hits the water, theoretically you could switch elements without the need for such trauma to instigate it."

Luke scratched his head. "I don't mean to be rude, but you don't really know anything about magic yet. How could you possibly know that?"

"It's just a gut feeling."

"Seriously?"

I nodded. "Yes, why?"

He slid off the bed and stood up. "If you can think of things like that when your magic is bound, what the hell are you going to be able to do when it's unbound?"

CHAPTER TWENTY-SEVEN

"It's going to hurt, Caitlyn. A lot." Mum's emerald eyes were full of worry. "I don't think you quite understand."

"Did it hurt when you bound me?"

"If you'd been awake, yes."

"Did you sneak into my room whilst I was asleep or something?"

Mum shook her head. "No. We cast a sleeping spell on you so you wouldn't wake up no matter what."

"Can't you do the same again?"

Mum shook her head. "You need to be awake at the end of it to take the potion."

I let out a long breath. "Ok, fine. Let's do it."

"Are you sure?"

I sighed. "Does my magic need unbinding?"

"I'm not sure if it's that much of a desperate need."

"Look, people know who I am and what supposed power I have, yes?"

Mum nodded.

"If I don't unbind myself, they'll most likely find a way to do it themselves. Am I wrong?"

"No. They will most likely kidnap you, torture you, and then make you agree to it."

Luke snorted. "They can try."

I smiled. "Going off that theory, surely I'm best to unbind myself and at least be half prepared for when they decide they want to drain my blood."

"They won't kill you," Hannah said. "If you die, your magic dies with you. They'll likely string you up and bleed you drip by drip so you replace what you lose constantly. Like a tap."

A ball of nausea swirled around in my stomach. "Thanks for that, Hannah."

She smiled. "You're welcome."

I looked at Mum and frowned. "I thought when a witch dies, their magic is released back into the universe to be recycled for future witches to be born with?"

Mum laughed. "You've met Keres."

"Yes…how do you know?"

"Because that's the crap she spins to keep her sheep following her. That is not what happens at all. When a rich person dies, what happens to their estate?"

"It's left to their relatives in the will."

Mum nodded. "Exactly. The family benefit from it. It doesn't get shared out between every other rich person on the planet, does it?"

"No."

"Same with magic. When a witch dies, their magic is dispersed amongst their surviving relatives. You will be noticing things now your dad has passed. That's his magic boosting yours."

"So why is Keres lying? She can't gain from sacrificing all those people."

"Oh, she can if they're relatives."

I frowned. "But how can she have that many relatives?"

"Breeding programmes."

"I'm sorry, what now?"

"It's a gig she's been running for years. She specifically matches witches together and encourages them to start a family. At some point in their bloodline, she will be linked. If the children are of power, she will keep them in the coven. If they're not, she blanks the minds of the parents and sends them out to live as normal humans. Then she will magically 'find them' with an illness, past the age where magic is useful, and sacrifice them."

"And no one suspects a thing?"

"Why would they? She gives them all a little power boost when a sacrifice is made. A temporary one mind, but because they feel the fizz in their veins they believe it's permanent."

I couldn't believe someone could be so manipulative and underhand. This wasn't right and if I had the power to do something, I damn well would.

I looked at Mum and said, "You need to unbind me. Now."

"We need to get the potion first."

"Where is it? What is this 'dark place never visited'?"

"It's open to interpretation. All it means is it needs to be stored somewhere it won't be disturbed until it's necessary."

"And where did you store it?"

Mum glanced at Luke and Hannah in turn then let out a big sigh. "Your father took the saying literally. There is a place not far from here that he never visited but really should have done. It was his dark place."

"Where?" Luke asked.

"It's near Goathland. Not many people have even heard of it. It's a tiny little village, well more like a hamlet actually. There's a waterfall there—"

"Beck Hole," Luke said.

Mum nodded. "Yes, how did you know?"

"I know every last inch of my family's territory. We have around five hundred and fifty-four square miles of it to be exact."

My jaw dropped. "How much?"

He grinned. "We have everything up to Guisborough, down to Scarborough, and over to Thirsk."

I pulled out my phone and fired up Google maps. "That's like the whole of the North York Moors National Park."

"We're a big family."

"But…but that's just greedy."

Luke laughed. "No, it's necessary. You'll find most werewolf families living in national parks. Anyway," he said, looking at my mum. "You were saying?"

"Your dad had a younger brother," Mum said, reaching across the table and grabbing my hand. "When they were ten and eight, they took a walk from Goathland down to Beck Hole waterfall. Roger was so excited by the place he went running through the water, tripped, and hit his head on a rock. Unfortunately, he died."

I sat in silence for a few minutes trying to wrap my head around this. I'd never once heard about Dad having a brother. I thought he was an only child.

"I don't know what to say. How come I never knew about this?"

"Your dad found it too hard to talk about. He kept all his pain and all his memories locked away in his mind and forced himself to pretend it never happened. He blamed himself for Roger's death. Said he should have been watching him closer."

"It was a terrible accident," I said. My heart was breaking all over again at the thought of Dad carrying guilt like that around with him for his entire life. "If it was going to happen, it was going to happen."

"Unfortunately, your father didn't see it like that."

In that moment, I wished I could have eased his pain in his final moments for him. Reassured him about any doubts or guilt he carried that he had no need to. That he could slip into eternal peace free from all worries.

"Was the potion hidden behind the waterfall inside a rock by any chance?" Luke asked.

Mum's face paled. "Yes…why?"

"It's not there anymore," Luke said. "But don't worry, I know where it is."

"What? What do you mean? You stole it? How did you even find it?" Mum said, standing up so fast her chair fell backwards.

"Calm down, Mum," I said, standing up. "Let him explain."

"This better be good," Mum said.

I coaxed her back down. She picked her chair up and sat down on it, glaring at Luke.

"I came across it not long after you'd put it there,"

Luke said. "I could smell it from ten miles away. It has a very distinctive aroma to it, and I knew whoever had gone to the trouble of hiding it there had done so for an important reason. I decided to take it and keep it for safe keeping. Whoever it belonged to would cross my path one day and here we are."

"That's a very risky game you played there," Mum said, narrowing her eyes at him. "That could have really backfired."

Luke shook his head. "I made sure our paths crossed," he said, looking at me.

"What do you mean? How did you know it was anything to do with me?" I asked him, totally confused.

"Because you have the same smell as whatever is in that bottle. It's highly unique."

"When did you know it was me?"

"Instantly. I'd caught your scent way before that. As soon as I smelled this at the waterfall, I had to find out what it was."

My head felt like it was going to explode. "Take me to get it," I said. "Now."

He held his hands up. "Ok, it's back at mine."

I stood up and rushed to the back door. "I mean it. Now."

He sighed, a small smile tugging at his lips. "Yes, Ma'am."

I ran outside to see that thankfully, he'd brought the BMW which meant a slightly faster drive back to his than if he'd brought the Audi. I didn't even wait for him to do his whole chivalrous routine. The car had keyless entry so the instant I knew he was within distance, I wrenched the door open and jumped in the passenger seat.

"You're mad, aren't you?" he asked, sliding into

the driver's seat.

"You think?"

"Nothing was going to happen to it, Cat. It's perfectly safe and has been for all these years."

"You didn't know that when you took it. You had no idea we were going to meet some day."

"Yes, I did."

"How?"

He shifted the car into gear and drove down the street. "I just did."

"Tell me."

"I have nothing to tell you, Cat. I got myself a job with your dad to ensure our paths would cross and some day you'd get the bottle back, whatever it was for."

A niggle in my gut told me he was partly telling the truth but not fully. "There's something more there, isn't there?"

His eyes flickered for a second, confirming my suspicions.

"Luke, tell me. Please."

"Now is not the time. Trust me."

"So there is something else?"

He sighed. "Yes, there is."

"You have to tell me now."

"No," he said, shaking his head. "I will tell you one day but not today."

"Why?"

"Because you've got enough going on right now without anything else thrown into the mix."

"And you get to decide that for me, do you? What I can and can't deal with?"

"That's not what I'm saying, Cat. You're taking it out of context."

My frustration reaching boiling point, I couldn't help but blow off some steam. "Am I? Am I really? Let's put things into perspective, shall we? My entire life I've been lied to and hidden away from some supernatural world where my own kind want to kill me, my….whatever the hell Marcus is, wants to drink me dry, and my best friend is some troll like bodyguard. I even killed my own Dad, Luke, so what on earth could you tell me that is going to add to more stress?"

He pursed his lips and kept his eyes fixed on the road ahead.

"Luke, hello?"

"I'm doing this for your own good," he said, his voice clipped.

"Oh, give it a rest. Just tell me."

"No, Caitlyn. That's the end of it."

"Luke, I swear to God if you don't tell me—"

"We're soulmates," he yelled. "Your smell is distinctive because you're my soulmate."

I froze. My heart stopped. My mind went blank. Soulmates? What? I flopped back in my seat feeling rather flummoxed. What was I supposed to do with that piece of information? Where did Marcus fit into all this exactly?

After a few minutes, I said, "You should have kept that to yourself."

I held my breath as I waited for his reaction. He looked at me out of the corner of his eye and then laughed. "You are something else."

"Thank you. I aim to please."

We turned off the main road and onto the track that led down to his house. The closer we came, the more my heart pounded. My life was locked up in a bottle in his home, had been all this time. I'd been around it so many times and never known any different.

He pulled up and switched the car off. I flung my seatbelt off and kicked the door open with my foot, sprinting towards his front door. I burst through the unlocked door and ran into the living room. Of course, I had no idea where he had put it or anything but all this nervous energy flitting around inside me made me need to do something.

"It's not in there," he said, heading upstairs.

I followed him upstairs, almost wanting to shout at him for not hurrying. He was waltzing around like he was taking a Sunday stroll.

He turned into one of the spare bedrooms, a draft of cold air rushing out when he opened the door. I expected to see a bed and furniture but instead I saw heaps of boxes, as if he were still moving in.

"This is all my parent's stuff," he said. "I can't put it in the loft. I find it soothing sometimes to go through it."

He picked his way through the dusty clutter to a bookshelf on the back wall. I made an attempt to follow him but a bunch of pictures peeking out the top of the box to my right caught my attention. I picked up a handful of them, musing at the children's smiling faces in various scenes from days on the beach to being on a set of swings.

"Don't," Luke said.

I looked up to see him coming back towards me, his face ashen grey and his hands reaching out for the photos.

"Awww, are you worried about me seeing your baby photos?" I said, teasing him.

"They're just very precious," he said, trying to take

them from me.

I moved them out of his way and took a step back. "I'm being careful with them."

He licked his lips and put his hands on his hips. "I'd just really rather you didn't."

I shuffled my way through the pictures and found a really cute one of a little boy with brown hair sat on an older man's shoulders.

"Oh look. Is this Meredith as a little boy?" I said, laughing.

"Cat, give me the pictures."

I turned my back to him and kept looking through them. As I uncovered the next one, I froze. My heart somersaulted over and over again. Staring back at me were Mirabelle and the man from my dream, the werewolf. The picture was old, the corners dog eared with a slight yellow tinge to it, but there was no mistaking them.

"Luke," I said, turning around shaking. The other pictures fell from my hand, cascading all around my feet as they landed on the floor. "Why do you have a picture of Marcus' mum?"

He looked at the floor, shuffling his feet. "They're my parents."

I looked up at him. "What?" I shook my head. "That's not possible. You said your mum was a witch."

"She is. She's also a vampire."

I tried to wrap my head around this, but I couldn't quite fathom it all for a good minute or more. "But that means Marcus is your half-brother."

Luke pulled his lips into a thin line. "I know."

A NOTE FROM THE AUTHOR

I hope you enjoyed Cat's story so far. If you did, I would be eternally grateful if you could leave a review to let others know how much you enjoyed it. Even one sentence is fine. Thank you so much!

If you want to follow me and keep up to date with all my latest goings on, visit www.cjlauthor.com and sign up for my newsletter, or look me up in the places below:
www.facebook.com/CJLaurenceAuthor
www.instagram.com/cjlauthor
https://www.bookbub.com/authors/c-j-laurence

I love hearing from my readers and will always reply to you!

ALSO BY THIS AUTHOR

Want and Need
Cowboys & Horses
Retribution
Unleashing Demons
Unleashing Vampires
The Red Riding Hoods – The Grim Sisters Book 1
Game Changer
Angel of the Crypt
The Twisted Tale of Saffron Schmidt
Love, Lies & Immortal Ties

Printed in Great Britain
by Amazon